BLIND FEAR

Also by Kingston Medland
and available from Headline Feature

The Edge
Shadow of the Soul
Until Dawn

BLIND FEAR

Kingston Medland

HEADLINE
FEATURE

First published in Great Britain in 1997 by
HEADLINE BOOK PUBLISHING

A HEADLINE FEATURE hardback

10 9 8 7 6 5 4 3 2 1

British Library Cataloguing in Publication Data

Medland, Kingston
Blind fear
1. English fiction – 20th century
I. Title
823.9'14 [F]

ISBN 0 7472 1940 0

Typeset by
CBS, Felixstowe, Suffolk

Printed and bound in Great Britain by
Mackays of Chatham PLC, Chatham, Kent

HEADLINE BOOK PUBLISHING
A division of Hodder Headline PLC
338 Euston Road
London NW1 3BH

To Catherine,
My Starlight.

لأن دائماً وإلى الأبد

Thanks to Andi, Joan and everybody at Headline for their constant work and support. Kingsley for his ever-valued criticism and pointers. Mark Parham for his valuable input. And Michael Alayan, for his linguistic expertise. Finally, you, the reader, for keeping the faith. Now hold tight, we're going to a dark place . . .

PROLOGUE

Hard Reign

The Lost Children – One

Ethan Wallace and Juliet Stevens were bad, all the way to the bone.

Barely out of their teens, they spent their days sleeping in cheap motels with dirty linen, and their nights traversing the good old United States of America. A young couple in love, making a dishonest living by robbing deserted gas stations, sometimes killing the clerk just for the thrill, to hear him beg or to watch his blood run in the rain.

Robbing and killing to finance their endless trek.

Juliet had been upset the first time she had killed a person. Four robberies into their violent spree, somewhere in the Midwest – place names didn't matter because they had all the time in the world – and the dumb-ass creep in the Harry Connick Jnr top, with his study books spread across the counter because he thought he was so clever, had struggled with her for the shotgun while Ethan cleaned out the cash register.

Well, poor 'Harry' wasn't so clever – even with the aid of all those books – because he didn't realise that if he met a speeding shell from her gun head on, he wouldn't be tickling the ivories again. Hell, he wouldn't even be breathing.

Only 'Harry' didn't die. Not right away. The shell had clipped the top of his head when the gun went off, shaving hair, skin and skull away, exposing a tiny part of his not-so-clever brain to the world. He fell backwards and then tried to crawl away. His movements were slow and every few seconds his head would jerk, as if suddenly yanked viciously to one side by an invisible hand. He made a pathetic mewling sound. Spittle and blood dribbled off his lip.

Juliet had remembered when she and Ethan were children,

3

growing up on the same street. There was a dead-end alley close to their homes and they used to box scavenging rats into a corner and take turns shooting at them with Ethan's .22. The first time she ever hit one of the rats, it was a plump little sucker that bled profusely. It shuffled about on the ground, disabled and looking confused. Ethan laughed at her horror, at the funny-looking rat, and then put a cap in its head. The little girl Juliet had cried long into the night and had been plagued by guilty nightmares of the rat coming back. Coming back for her with its needle fangs and tiny bite . . .

'Harry', dying on the floor, reminded her of that poor rat – the first living creature she had ever killed. She felt tears in her eyes; mesmerised, she watched him struggle to breathe, and then Ethan pumped three bullets into his back. Boom. Boom. Boom. Like the thunder. She flinched with each crash.

'Guess he won't play the piano so good now!' Ethan laughed wildly.

Juliet smiled, her sadness quickly forgotten. Ethan always had something funny to say at the right moment. She could always depend on him to cheer her. He was so cool.

'I love you,' she whispered over the bloody corpse.

He blew her a kiss and stooped down to the body.

'Goddamn mess,' he mumbled, reaching into 'Harry's' pocket for his wallet. He opened it and looked disappointed. '*This* is your money. *This* is what you were protecting. You died for five lousy bucks. Stupid shit.'

Ethan kicked the body with disgust and stuffed the wallet into his pocket anyway. 'Grab me some of them cookies, Juliet. We got to get us out of here.'

That was five months ago.

Four dead bodies and eleven robberies later, Juliet lay in the bed of the latest motel they were calling home, staring at the cracked ceiling. A spider was halfway across it, trapped in a column of light from outside.

She had just woken from a dream that she had often. They had a house. They were married. And they had children . . . She smiled at the fading memory. A sweet boy and an angelic little girl. The perfect family.

She looked at Ethan, bathed in the glow of headlights as a semi rumbled by in the night. Startled by the shifting patterns across the ceiling, the spider scurried for a shadowy corner, the sanctity of its web. The light vanished and Ethan snored on. Loudly. She sighed. He always seemed to fall asleep after loving her. Sometimes she wanted him to just hold her a while and share her dream. *The* dream. Ethan was such a good man. She was sure he'd understand.

'Ethan?' She shook him. 'Ethan – you awake?'

Still no response, but his snoring had ceased and she knew he was faking.

'I bet I can wake you,' Juliet giggled, arousing him with her hand.

'That feels good,' he moaned quietly.

She figured it would be best to hit him with the proposition, the idea of having children and settling down, while he was excited. 'Ethan, I love you and I want us to have a baby.'

Ethan felt his erection melting. 'What did you just say?' he whispered.

'Two,' she said dreamily. 'A boy and a girl. And a house. We can sleep and shop – pay for stuff like real people. I want to do the whole family deal.' She continued to use her hand, but there was little reaction now. 'Ethan, what's wrong?'

'You sure know how to kill a mood,' he grumbled. 'Juliet, we're street-trash. Gutter-bugs. How can we raise a family? Where could we get a house? I mean, don't you ever think before you start flapping your lips?'

'You don't have to be nasty. I've thought a lot about this. I look at children and they're so cute. They make me smile inside, like you do all the time. Wouldn't it be fun if we had children of our own?'

'Juliet, kids aren't pets. They're a full-time occupation. Fun is *not* how it would be. We rob people, honey. We kill them and drift to where the breeze takes us. How could we raise children? We couldn't afford it.'

Juliet began to cry softly. 'If we don't have children,' she sniffed, 'then I don't want to be your girl.'

She rolled away from him. He let her sulk for a few minutes, thinking about the situation. It would be cool to be a father, he supposed. A child would be somebody to carry on their name and continue their legacy. And if they ever did get bored with the brats – well, they would just dump them somewhere. Nobody would ever know.

'Honey, let's talk about it,' he said, warming to the idea. 'Where would we live?'

'Remember my Uncle Benny who lives on the farm – the one with no animals because he got old and sold his livestock when Aunt Gertie died? Well, he has nobody to love him now, and the house is empty and quiet, so we could just . . . *kill him*,' she whispered, looking around cautiously. 'Nobody would notice he was gone, I promise – and then we could fill that big, old house with joy and love again.'

'We could do that,' Ethan admitted casually. It would even give them somewhere regular to live.

'I look at pregnant women and wonder what it would be like, to carry a life inside me,' Juliet murmured, her eyes glazed over. 'But I don't want to ruin my figure with all that extra weight,' she worried. 'Or to get a bad back and throw up all the time. Or have swollen ankles and stretchmarks.'

'That's all part of being pregnant, Juliet. It comes with the territory. But you're right; I don't want no fat chick to love,' he informed her.

'And I don't want to be no fat chick,' Juliet confessed. 'I like my figure just fine, and so do you.'

'So do I,' he agreed, kissing her shoulder.

'We could adopt,' he suggested after a minute.

'That's stupid. People like us aren't allowed to adopt children.'

'Then we could take one.' His eyes glimmered in the moonlight.

The spider was venturing bravely out onto the ceiling again, but Juliet didn't notice. She was staring deep into Ethan's serious eyes.

'You mean kidnap? That's a bad thing,' she reminded him.

'I don't mean kidnap, I mean steal. No ransom letters or calls that can be traced. No intention of ever giving back. We could have two babies of our own – a boy and a girl – and you don't even have to get fat. Let's do it!'

6

'Yeah!' she screamed, delighted. 'Ethan, you're the best guy a girl could ever have. You're so romantic.'

In the darkness, Ethan sighed. 'Good night, Juliet,' he yawned.

'Do you promise about the babies?' she asked.

'Sweetheart, I'd give you the whole world if I could, with a little ribbon tied on top.' He kissed her slowly. 'Two babies are no big deal.'

The dream took a while to realise. Ethan said they had to take things slowly and not make any mistakes.

A year later Uncle Benny was dead and buried in the mud where he used to keep his pigs. After watching the sad old coot for a month, Ethan had decided he was as lonely as the last dodo on the planet. And then there were none, he grinned, finishing the burial. Juliet was right; nobody was ever going to miss him.

They practised buying groceries – actually paying for them, without killing the clerk. Indeed, when they robbed or murdered now it was always out of state.

Kill, Juliet corrected thoughtfully. It was never murder. That was a bad thing. Killing was what you did with a horse when it had a bad leg or was sick and miserable and needed shooting. Juliet had learned that on Uncle Benny's farm when she was a little girl and the place was a crawling menagerie of creatures and critters. Ethan told her that all their kills were righteous; the people were lame, and as such they were providing a service. From that perspective, she could always look a person in the sad eye and pull the trigger without concern. They were going to a better world.

Ethan and Juliet were expecting, so the right thing to do was decorate a room for the children. They did this with much zest and zeal, excitement growing by the day, the moment of delivery coming closer and closer, until . . .

The night nurse was dead. The little side-ward with its dozen occupied bassinets was silent. All the newborn babies slept.

They had spent months scouting out hospitals in small towns across state, before Ethan had decided that this one would adequately serve their needs.

Even as they sneaked between the rows of cradles, glancing at each child, not a single baby stirred. This relieved Ethan. If one of the infants cried, it would probably wake them all up. And that would not do.

Gently he plucked a helpless baby boy from his cocoon of soft blankets. *Dominick Rain* was the name on his tiny wrist-tag.

'Come to Papa,' he whispered, holding the little one close to his chest. Then: 'Hurry the fuck up,' he hissed at Juliet, who was now on the far side of the ward. Another nurse could appear at any second. 'Just grab one of the little suckers and let's get out of here.'

Juliet bent over a sleeping girlchild. 'Hi, *Lorna Cole*,' she whispered, 'I'm your new mommy.'

One year into a normal – though secluded – life and Juliet's eyesight began to wane. She told Ethan, who was a great father and even changed diapers – God, she hated that smell, hated the children for creating it, *hated* the motherhood that had made her miserable – but he said that because of their dwindling savings, the babyclothes and babyfood and all, they couldn't afford an eye-check.

Juliet mourned for the early days of their partnership, which had been so happy and carefree. Parenthood wasn't all it was cracked up to be. She decided to give it a year or two longer, or maybe just a few months, and then tell Ethan that she had made a mistake; she didn't want the children. Dominick and Lorna were nothing but a burden.

The next time they needed some money, Ethan made a point of killing a sweet teenager with a delicate pair of stylish wire-rims, while Juliet reluctantly stayed home and looked after the babies. It was no fun and she was bored by it. They were pod people. Their cuteness factor had lasted all of a week.

Ethan gift-wrapped the spectacles and gave them to her on her birthday. He was so romantic, she cooed, not noticing the tiny smear of blood across the left lens which he hadn't bothered to wipe away.

But her eyesight continued to deteriorate until one day, two years later, she blinked, and could no longer see.

Juliet was blind.

Ethan thought about leaving her, but couldn't do it. True love – what a pain in the butt. He tried to leave her one night, but spent the lonely hours missing all he cared for in the world. Come sunrise, he was asleep at her side.

'I love you,' he whispered, waking with the dawn. 'I have an idea.'

She listened.

'It will be just like the old days,' he promised in conclusion.

'It sounds perfect,' she told him after they made love. 'When can we start?'

The Curse

Sixteen years ago . . .

Tabitha Warner noticed two things when she opened the door of her small ground-floor apartment, both of them unusual.

The first was the heat that washed over her as she stepped into the little entrance lobby.

Every morning, before she left for her daily walk in Starlight Park, she opened a small window off the living room to ventilate the stuffy shoebox-sized rooms. Upon her return, she was greeted by a cool breeze, her apartment pleasantly air-conditioned. For this purpose she also had a small electric fan which pivoted left to right, sending comforting turbulence into the room.

Tabitha hesitated in the doorway. The air now was thick and hot. She wondered if it was her imagination, but she felt sure that if she entered the room the heat would suffocate her.

The second was that Pugsley, her playful kitten, was nowhere *to be seen*, she thought sadly, having still not come to terms with her loss of sight. Normally, the critter was at her feet, soft fur on her legs, mewling for attention.

'Pugsley?' she asked, still in the doorway.

She felt uneasy. Something was not right.

Street sounds suddenly filtered in for a second as another person entered the building. She cocked her head, listening intently. Somebody was approaching – a heavyset man, his breathing laboured. She drowned in the noise, claustrophobia swallowing her so that when the man grabbed her arm she jerked around, rigid with fear.

'Hey, Tabby, relax. It's only me – Bob,' the man told her.

10

'Oh hi, Bob,' Tabitha greeted him, suddenly feeling foolish for jumping.

'You OK?'

'Yeah, sure. I was just spooking myself,' she said uncertainly.

'Want me to go inside and take a look?' he offered.

She smiled sweetly. He sounded like a knight in shining armour, escorting and protecting his princess. The imagery made her feel more foolish and she stifled a laugh.

'No, thanks. I'll be all right. How far did you manage today? I can smell the cigarettes on your breath. You always stop for smokes.'

'About ten miles. I'll never be in shape for the company marathon. I don't know why they didn't just have a charity pie-eating contest or something,' Bob laughed. 'Talking of food, are we still eating together tomorrow?'

'As long as I'm buying,' Tabitha promised.

'Good girl,' he whispered, lightly kissing her on the cheek. 'I wouldn't have it any other way.'

She listened to his footfalls fade as he jogged across the hall-way, and waited for the swing door to *hush* shut. He always took the stairwell because he got bad claustrophobia in the elevators.

Shaking her head, Tabitha entered her apartment and closed the door. She placed the white cane against the wall and walked confidently down the narrow hall. Here, in her home, her private sanctuary away from the loud world, it didn't matter that she was blind. The rest of society couldn't intrude; it was her domain.

'Pugsley? You back there?' Tabitha asked, walking through the main living room and into the bedroom. She kicked her shoes off and placed them on the left side of her bed, with the rest. She had learned the hard way that order was important.

'Pugsley?'

She grinned, revealing perfect teeth. Her cat had obviously jumped out of the window to go on an adventure and caught the latch, causing it to fall shut. That explained the heat and her missing friend. She forgot all about the fan.

'How did you plan on getting back in? You stupid pussy,' she chuckled, and moved out of the room, unaware of the man staring

11

at her, so close, holding a pair of her panties, sniffing them for her scent . . .

Tabitha turned at the faint noise. 'Is somebody there?' she asked, sensing slight movement. Sweat sprang to the surface of her skin. 'Bob – is that you? It's not funny.'

Her heartbeat echoed through her body. She decided to call the police, a loud klaxon pulsing a warning through her system.

She turned to the telephone on the wall.

The receiver was snatched from Tabitha's hand and a strong, tightly balled fist pushed her back against the wall. Undeniably male. Held her there and rammed into her chest, seemed determined to force through her stomach.

The terror Tabitha felt – a soundless, dry scream breaking her lips – was a stronger feeling than her first experience of blindness, the sudden panic and confusion as she realised she would never see again.

After an eternity of futile struggle, the hand let go and she bolted across the room. Her desperate flight only lasted a second before she stumbled over a small glass table and lay winded on the ground. It shouldn't have been there; he had moved the table to confuse her.

'Why don't you look where you're going?' the intruder sneered.

Tabitha crawled away from the voice, completely disorientated now. Her legs hurt and she felt broken glass cutting her palms. She came to a wall and let out a sob, realising she no longer knew where the exit was. *She had become lost in her own apartment.*

In a building several blocks away from Tabitha Warner's apartment, the blind psychic Faith Gallagher was being interviewed by officers from the Denver Police Department. She had recently volunteered her services to help catch the killer who was stalking the city's blind women. So far, three bodies had been found.

Upon the discovery of the first, due to the state of mutilation, a serial unit had been set up, headed by Detectives Chris Slater and Will Bradley. It was not long before another body was found. And three months ago, the third.

Now the blind community – particularly the women – was living in fear. The police were advising them not to go out alone. Some were afraid to use their canes or guide dogs, figuring it would signpost them to the killer.

Faith suddenly began to tremble, her skin turning deathly pale.

'What's wrong, Faith? What's happening?' These were the concerned tones of Detective Will Bradley. He was only a young detective, but already he had mournful eyes after cleaning up the dead for far too long.

'The kitten is dead and the young woman – her name is Tabitha Warner – is running out of time.'

'Jesus,' Will exclaimed and grabbed his radio. 'Chris, she's tuned in to the next killing.' He looked back to Faith. 'I need an address, Faith. Where is she?'

'She's on the ground floor. It's an apartment block – number two hundred and fifty-four, on Fortieth. God, please hurry Will! She's going to die like the others!'

He quickly relayed the information to Slater, and then began rapping orders out to the officers around him. We're going to save this one, he fleetingly thought. 'Let's move!'

Bradley was a good man in a world gone bad, turned to shit. His superiors believed he was one of the best, that he and Detective Slater both had the potential to go all the way. To turn things around.

Faith began to convulse at the horrific acts she was witnessing and Will held her softly. Her second sight, cruelly given to one without the power of vision, was to Faith Gallagher a curse. I have helped the police before, she thought, and after each time I say I will never go back. Yet sometimes I believe I may be of use, that I can make a difference.

Will Bradley feels the same way, and it is this forlorn hope that keeps him on the Force; that he can save those who otherwise might die.

Now: 'Strong hands are pulling her arms back. He binds them tight; she can't move.' Faith swallowed deeply and then continued, rubbing her wrists. She could actually feel the thin rope, the burning terror. 'She struggles with the binding . . .'

She held on to Will Bradley's hand like the dying woman clinging to life. 'He's gagged her. She's trying to scream, but can't. Hurry,

Bradley! Get somebody out there. You have to stop this! He has a knife! He's cutting at her blouse.' Faith flinched and held her chest at the position of each wound. 'It's glancing off her skin. He hasn't seriously cut her yet. She might still live! Be there now!'

'Break the connection,' Bradley told her. 'You're too deep. The unit is close. Get out of there!'

'*I can't*. She's naked now. Her breathing is ragged. She's shivering in the heat. His breath is suddenly close. It smells of mint.' Suddenly, after a pause as she appeared to listen intently, she told him calmly: 'He wants to play a game, Will.'

'Faith, are you into that creep's head?' Bradley demanded.

'See if you can get his address,' a remaining officer suggested urgently. 'We can pick this sick fuck up later if we don't catch him at the scene.'

'Forget it, Faith. Get the hell out of there. It's too dangerous. *Now!*' Bradley shouted emotionally, grabbing her arms and shaking her body.

There was a long silence as Faith collapsed back into her chair and witnessed Tabitha's final struggle to escape the cold and unfamiliar and dark, dark place that had once been her home.

'It was over very quickly,' Faith told them on a sob. 'She's dead, the poor darling. But he's not left yet. He's doing something. The mint . . . I don't know.'

'What did he do?' Bradley asked. 'What's the game?'

But Faith only shuddered, her skin suddenly cold, her heart freezing. She would not share what had just happened with Bradley. She had had an actual vision, and prayed that it would never happen again. She had actually seen it, without depending on her empathic skills of detecting emotion.

I am looking down. Her bound and naked body has been eviscerated. There is blood everywhere, so much blood . . . The door suddenly bursts open and I recognise the voice of Detective Slater.

'Faith, talk to me. What's wrong?' Bradley enquired gently.

I can still see the naked, dead woman, Slater standing over her. It is crystal clear, as though I am watching with my own eyes and I am not blind.

A curse, a curse, a curse.

'He's gone,' Faith sobbed. 'They were too late.'

PART ONE

Blind Faith

Release

One week ago . . .

The package was exactly where Lorna Cole – his lawyer, sister and lover – had said it would be. Dominick Rain ripped into the thick brown envelope, eagerly checking the contents and holding them close to his chest. The neighbourhood was not the nicest in Los Angeles, and he didn't want to get mugged on his first day out of the Orange County Facility for the Criminally Insane.

The package held two thousand dollars in bills of a hundred and less. He didn't check the money. It was a gift from Lorna, whom he hadn't seen in years. During his stay in the asylum – after being transferred from a prison over a decade ago – they had decided it would be better if she didn't visit, except for professional purposes when she was acting as his lawyer.

He removed a small card from the envelope. It contained the printed address of a hotel and a room number scribbled in her writing. He touched it, touched her fingers holding the pen . . . She would contact him there soon.

He re-sealed the package and stowed it inside his jacket. Catching his reflection in a car wing-mirror, he touched his face and grinned. He was no longer wanted by the police. He was free, his debt supposedly paid to society via all his years' incarceration . . . A debt that could never be paid to all his victims, nor to their families and friends.

He could walk down the street as he was now and not worry about the siren-song of the police, aware that he was no longer being hunted for his sins.

He wanted to climb the highest mountain, go to the roof of the tallest building, and yell it to the world. Free at last, after all the years of claustrophobia, the cell closing in on him like the encroaching walls *of the cellar . . . only then he had Lorna's soft touch and friendship. He had not been alone.* In prison the nights were worst; when the dark accompanied the suffocation, and the violent penetration of depraved men, repeatedly raping him, left him crying on his bunk for the companionship of the woman who was still so willing to help him.

Jesus, it had been horrible. And people were supposed to become rehabilitated in that Hell. If he had gone in a nun, he would have come out ready to cut throats! The fine scars on his left cheek and chin were lifetime reminders of the time he had spent there.

In the asylum there were white walls and white bars and no windows. He used to imagine the purest white snow and told the doctors what he suspected they wanted to hear, until they decided that they had heard enough.

A black and white cruiser drove by, one of the uniforms giving him a cursory glance. He shivered; he didn't feel safe. But they were not searching for him. He was no longer the hunted. Not yet, he smiled.

Day One – 0917

The Act

The tall woman who stood before the Hollywood office of private investigator Will Bradley had a body that could melt ice. Her head was crowned by a short crop of blonde hair. She hated it, far preferred her normal cascade of brunette locks, but it was important that Bradley not remember her. Even though they hadn't seen each other for over a decade, the attempt at disguise was a necessary precaution.

All those years ago, they had stood on opposing sides of a courtroom, she as a leading defence attorney; he as a witness for the prosecution, and already at the end of his short police career. The case concluded when her client, Dominick Rain, her brother and her only true love, was sent to a maximum security penitentiary. The only thing saving him from Death Row had been the mitigating circumstances surrounding his horrible crimes – the serial killer's sad personal history, which led to his eventual internment at the Orange County Facility for the Criminally Insane.

Lorna Cole studied her reflection in the office window. She hated her hair, and felt sleazy in a low-cut outfit one of the many hookers she chose to defend would be proud to wear, but knew she had to use any and every advantage to distract the sad, lonely Bradley from the facts. If that included fucking the divorcé on his desk, then so be it.

She was wearing more make-up than usual, and blue contact lenses to disguise the natural colour of her green eyes.

He must not remember her.

Fifteen years ago she had let Dominick down badly. Now he had finally been released, and she would do anything for him. She wouldn't fail him again.

* * *

'Yeah, I know,' Will Bradley was saying as the blonde stranger walked into his office. Don't bother knocking, he thought, just come on in. But when he saw her stunning figure, he didn't mind. She sat on the opposite side of Will's desk, looking over the muddled contents. Sit right down, why don't you? Make yourself at home. Then: 'No, that's not how it went,' he stammered defensively. 'Nothing like that. You told me to follow your wife.'

Will held the receiver away from his mouth as a tirade of abuse came down the line. 'Angry husband,' he shrugged, and then turned his attention back to the telephone. 'I strongly deny that,' Bradley spat vehemently. 'I was watching her all the time . . . but from the inside of her bedroom.'

Bradley grinned, but the woman across the desk didn't smile. Lorna thought she saw a flash of the old, arrogant Bradley. Perhaps he was not as big a loser as she'd been led to believe. She wondered if it had been a mistake to come here, but then decided the charming smile had actually been the pathetic leer of a desperate man.

No sense of humour, Will reflected, studying the gorgeous woman for a moment, and continued to doodle on a sheet of paper. It was a sketch of Dr Beverly Crusher from *Star Trek: The Next Generation*. She was wearing a skimpy outfit of his own design.

'Yeah, that's right. I provided you with evidence that she was sleeping around. I'll expect the cheque in the mail, OK, or you'll be hearing from my lawyer. Is that a fact? I gave you photographic evidence and I can supply carnal knowledge. Nice little mole she has, down there. Yeah, and fuck you too,' Bradley concluded and slammed the telephone down. 'He hung up when I mentioned the cheque,' Bradley smiled. 'You don't think I would really treat a client like that, do you?'

Beverly Crusher finished, he began to work on a similar portrait of Counsellor Deanna Troi as he listened to the woman.

'Just their wives,' Lorna presumed.

The man Lorna used to know as Detective Bradley, her arch nemesis on many cases before helping to steal her lover away and lock him up, had changed. He had become a shadow of his former self, a burned-out cliché striving to prove his individuality,

20

that he still had something unique and of value to offer the world. She conceded that he was only slightly overweight, but he *was* a wreck.

'Touché,' Bradley said, closing a file on his desk. 'Another happy customer.'

'I'm sure his wife was satisfied,' Lorna offered, realising that she was going to have to communicate at the ex-cop's pace and not her own. She didn't know how long she could suffer this idle banter. She had to get out as quickly as possible, lest he recognise her. She also despised the man before her, didn't care to be around him longer than she had to.

'You know, you're probably right.'

Lorna would normally have used the detective team retained by the law firm in which she was a partner. She was aware that if the other lawyers saw her dressed like this they would be horrified, although the younger ones might be turned on. They would never let her near any clients, whereas she normally led all prospective courtships. Any detectives she approached from their own staff would have to file reports, claim expenses; something would have been discovered and complications would have arisen.

Instead, a month ago she had asked her lover – FBI Agent Jack Ramsey – to locate former Denver detective, Will Bradley.

The irony was delicious. The night Jack had given her the address, told her that Bradley was now a private investigator, she had made love to him, pumping and grinding until he was exhausted, scratching viciously, laughing deliriously. She felt like she was high, would do anything to maintain the feeling. One of Faith Gallagher's guardians from all those years ago, would now lead Dominick to her so that he could destroy her, finally taste the sweet vengeance which had flavoured his existence for the past two decades.

Then she and Dominick could finally be together, living in peace and tranquillity. Once Faith was dead, he had promised, he would end his legacy of terror.

'I need you to find somebody for me,' Lorna told Bradley.

'Who are you looking for?'

'A woman.'

'Aren't we all,' Bradley said, not quite managing to hide his morose tone behind a quiet laugh. Lorna wondered if he was still hurting after his messy divorce, but that was years ago. Or perhaps he still harboured feelings for Faith Gallagher.

'I need you to be subtle. No flyers or posters. Just locate her and tell me where she is.'

'Who is she?'

'Her name is Faith,' Lorna informed the ex-cop she loathed. She stood up and dropped an envelope onto the desk. 'That's a retainer and a photograph, with all the details. I'm sorry I don't have a more recent picture. I've left a number where I can be contacted.'

'Very cloak and dagger,' Bradley said. 'I'll remember to put on my raincoat before I call.'

Lorna was at the door, thought she was going to make it out easy as pie, when Bradley called her back.

'Hey, lady, this isn't the movies. You don't even know my fees,' he told her.

But that was the least important of his questions; the rest were forgotten when she turned. She had opened her blouse a couple of buttons and he couldn't help but stare. It had been a long time for Will Bradley, not counting a couple of close encounters with the wives of clients. He might still have the charisma and wit, maybe even the charm, but he was carrying a few more pounds since his days on the Force and the ladies no longer bothered to look twice.

'The money should cover your fees. If not, let me know the difference once you have found her and I'll write a cheque,' Lorna smiled, aware of where his attentions were.

Bradley looked her over. She might be able to thaw out the produce in the freezer compartments of a supermarket, but she looked as if her cheque would bounce like a tennis ball.

'I'll settle for cash,' Bradley told her, and to stop himself staring at her cleavage, he opened the envelope, promptly dropping it when he saw the photograph.

'Faith!' he exclaimed, shocked.

Lorna smiled secretly. There had been talk all those years ago that Bradley had a thing for Faith Gallagher, but never knew how to approach her on an intimate level, and then, after he'd almost let her die, he'd found solace in the bottle and love in the arms of the next woman he'd slept with. Did he still pine for her during the long and lonely nights?

'You . . . you know my Faith?' Lorna stammered, playing him like a fiddle.

'A long time ago,' Bradley murmured, aware that if he found her he would be facing the guilt and the demons of his past all over again. He cleared his throat. 'What's your relation to her?'

'I was adopted as a baby.' Lorna let a few tears wet her cheeks. 'I've just found out that Faith is my sister.'

Bradley nodded. Back when he was a young detective in Denver he'd run checks on Faith Gallagher when she had come forward with information regarding the killer of blind people, Dominick Rain. Faith had lost her sight, her parents and her little brother when she was seven, in a car accident. No existing relatives could be found, so Faith was raised in the Radford & Doyle Institute while her baby sister had been adopted.

'Will you help me find my sister?' Lorna asked.

Bradley swallowed deeply. He had lived with the guilt for far too long; it was a burden he needed to rid from his heart. He nodded. 'I'll find Faith for you.'

After Lorna had left, Bradley contemplated the past for a long while, tears in his eyes. He blinked them back and checked the rest of the envelope's contents. He almost fell out of his seat. Two thousand dollars in cash was inside.

'I think I might close early today,' he announced to the empty office.

He descended the stairs to the streets of Hollywood, a town where dreams really could come true, he decided, for here was his own second chance. An opportunity to atone for his mistakes in Denver and an occasion to see Faith Gallagher once more; perhaps clean up his act and even dare tell her of his love for her.

The Big Wheel – One

Faith Gallagher sat typing at her desk, listening to the delicate sounds of the wind chimes Albert Dreyfuss had hung on her porch. A light wind blew in from the open door and she felt it caress her neck.

I have not had a vision for over a year . . . until this morning, she typed, her fingers flying over the especially adapted keyboard.

I woke and my mind was spinning. At first, I believed it to be the fragments of a dream, and then I saw that it was actually a giant wheel turning, revolving a thousand times a second.

I believe it to be symbolic of the nightmare curse which has plagued me since my blindness. It had been lying dormant within, yet all the time it was living, breathing, existing. Evolving.

I realise now that no matter how far I run, how deep I hide, my beating heart will always be living fuel for its haunting flame. I thought I had found sanctuary in this small desert town called Cradle, but I now know that peace is an illusion I shall never experience.

The Big Wheel rolls on.

In recent times the curse has matured, offered me more control, instead of the painful flashes of the early years. But the history of all that . . . horror . . . is recorded previously in this journal. I welcome my mind's quick dismissal of the memories.

I hate the curse; wish I could douse its eternal fire.

I abhor this power which some people call a gift. Others claim it has saved lives, given them hope. Let the Fates bestow it upon them and relieve me of my burden, for it is an affliction!

The Big Wheel keeps on turning . . .

I don't know what the image means. I may never decipher it.

But now and for ever, the Big Wheel keeps on turning, the curse evolving. Living within me.

Faith Gallagher stopped typing and stepped out on her porch – not using her cane in the familiar surroundings. The wind blew her hair back as it gusted. She looked beautiful in the severe drought, a matriarch to the golden landscape around her. Her skin was still smooth, silky, defying the aging process, fighting on, and her lips could open into a gorgeous smile; yet, for now, they remained thin, a grim expression burrowing into her elegant features.

Faith could not see the gathering clouds above her, but instinctively knew that a storm was coming. She stood in a trance then, suddenly captured by the Big Wheel, spinning and spinning, its revolutions seeming to feed the power. She remained on the porch for nearly five minutes, until she heard the sound of a motorbike coming down the lane to her home, a lonely sentinel on the desolate landscape.

It was Albert. Faith was not expecting him, but often he came down from his unusual home just to check on her. She always chastised him, told him she was not handicapped and could exist without the nurturing of a Hell's Angel softie.

'Hey, you talk to me like that and I'll bring the gang around to trash your place,' Albert had joked one day in his boyish tones. She had never asked his age, but was sure he was no older than twenty-five. Probably a few years younger. Just a kid.

Secretly, she liked his company greatly, and it was the surprise visits that brought her the most pleasure.

The engine cut off, and she heard his boots on the dusty ground.

'Hello, Albert,' she greeted him, the vision of the Big Wheel gone, leaving her only the blanket darkness of an abyss without daylight.

'Some bad weather is heading our way,' Albert commented, approaching her.

'I know,' she nodded, not yet aware that her inner vision of the Big Wheel was a warning of events that would shatter the seclusion and peace she had found in the once-quiet town of Cradle.

Walking The Stars

Will Bradley wandered down Hollywood Boulevard from his rundown office.

'Hey, Will!' called an old lady, sat across the street. 'You out chasing ambulances again?'

'Lawyers chase ambulances, Miss Garibaldi,' he informed her, as he did most afternoons, and smiled, adding inaudibly: 'I just chase the neglected wives of clients.'

'You have a good day!' she called after him.

'I'll bring you a coffee regular when I come back,' he told her.

Down the pavement, dodging the many tourists who were staring wide-eyed at the bronzed stars in the ground, unaware of the grimy reality of Hollywood, Will spotted Mitchell Ford close to Mann's Chinese Theatre.

The tourists didn't realise that this town was like every other one. It was a dark place, Will thought. He'd seen murder, robbery, blackmail and bribery, all kinds of human suffering during his time here. Hollywood could be any town, anywhere, except for the dream factor which drew so many into its inescapable lair.

'I'm looking for a woman,' Bradley told Mitchell Ford when he reached the aging hippie trying to hawk his goods to passing tourists.

Ford had set up a creaking desk on the sidewalk of the stars. For a second the man watched pedestrians as they stared at the dirty, decorated pavement. A couple of people even had a bucket of soapy water and were scrubbing clean the stars they had adopted of their favourite actors and actresses. Others studied the footprints and handprints, paw-prints, even robot-prints, set in concrete outside Mann's Chinese Theatre, beneath the beautiful pagoda. Photographs were snapped amidst happy smiles.

26

Nobody paid any attention to Ford or his wares on the table.

'Aren't we all,' Ford responded, finally acknowledging his friend. 'Would you look at these people. They don't even realise that an actor can buy his own place on the Walk of Fame. Sure, sometimes it's an honour, but a lot of the time it's vanity, I tell you.'

Long ago, when Bradley had mentioned to his friends back in Denver that he was thinking of moving to Dreamland, his Desk Sergeant, an old-timer named McCoy, had told him: 'You do make it out there, look up a guy called Mitchell Ford. He was a detective from these parts. A good man like yourself.'

Bradley smiled at the retired detective who had become a close friend. Ford was wearing a baseball cap on top of long grey hair tied back in a ponytail. His face was wrinkled, ravaged by time. As one smoke ended, he lit another.

'Guess you still haven't sold your screenplay,' Will presumed.

Everybody has a screenplay in Hollywood. Everybody has an audition to go to, a pitch to sell. A line to run. Everybody wants to be in the movies. Except Will didn't need fame or glory to feel alive. His heartbeat was enough to drive him forward.

'Don't ask. Hey, how about this? You rummage through these clothes and make like there is some good stuff here while we talk, try to rustle me up some business,' Ford suggested. 'One good ex-cop to another.'

'I didn't know you used to be a *good* cop,' Will joked and picked up a T-shirt with a print of Tom Cruise staring off the front. 'I got a client, Mitchell, and—'

'He isn't married, is he?'

Will didn't wonder how Ford had heard about his fling so soon. The man had connections everywhere and was a valuable source of information on most jobs the private investigator ever had. 'No. *She* isn't married, I don't think. I don't even know her name,' Will whispered, slightly anxious. He had been blinded by the fast buck, the sure thing of money in his hand . . . but mostly by thoughts of Faith Gallagher, which he now sought to avoid. 'She wants me to find a woman.'

'Just so long as she isn't married,' Ford smiled. 'How many divorces are you trying to cause, anyway?'

'I sleep with the wife of one client and all of a sudden I'm—'

'Is this polyester?' a large, older woman interrupted rudely. They both turned. She was overly made-up with a garish hairstyle. She picked up a sweater featuring David Duchovny and Gillian Anderson – alias Fox Mulder and Dana Scully from *The X-Files*. 'What do you think? A girl like me and Spooky Mulder?'

Ford and Bradley looked at each other incredulously, and then Mitchell turned his attention to the woman, thinking that poor David Duchovny should be pitied if this is what his average adoring female fan looked like.

'No,' the vendor said, responding to all her questions. 'Only the finest materials here, the softest silks and—'

'Cut the crap, sonny. I used to have my own spiel when I worked for the bus company over in Manhattan. Polyester makes me itch like a raccoon.'

'There's no polyester,' Ford lied and the woman handed over a ten-dollar bill and walked away. 'She'll be *itching like a raccoon* for weeks,' he grinned. 'Ford's law: Don't give attitude to the man behind the counter because he'll always come out on top. So, who are you looking for?'

Will pulled the photograph from his pocket and Ford studied it.

'Her name is Faith Gallagher,' Bradley informed him. 'I remember her from an old case. She's blind. I know that she came out this way, made a killing from her story. You've had this table longer than they've been making movies in this town. What do you know?'

Mitchell handed the picture back. 'It'll cost you.'

'It always does. Anybody listening would believe we are not friends. What's the deal?'

'Two sweat tops.'

'Come on, Mitchell. The last time I bought one of your shirts it fell apart in the wash,' Bradley haggled.

A woman looking at a Brad Pitt T-shirt put it down and walked away.

'Will you please keep it quiet.'

'OK, OK,' Bradley stammered, hands open in a gesture of supplication. 'How much is this gonna cost me?'

'Thirty dollars a garment.'

28

'What? The sign says: *Fifteen for one, two for twenty,*' Bradley complained. 'How about a concession for an old buddy off the Force?'

'I know what the sign proclaims, I wrote it. But you and your big mouth just cost me a customer.'

Bradley handed the cash over and grabbed two sweaters randomly. He already had a closet full of clothing from previous encounters with his friend. One of these days he was going to clear it all out and pass it on to the nice people at Helping Hands. Even they would probably turn the sweat tops away.

'What did she end up doing? Acting in cheap porn films?' Bradley enquired, deliberately hiding his true emotions.

'I see your viewing habits haven't changed,' Ford observed insidiously. 'Besides, you're way off base. She just found herself an agent, made the one deal and then got out of town. You need to talk to Lo Goldman. Tough bitch – but a good person to have standing at the plate if she likes your material. She represented Faith Gallagher. Contact either Goldman or the Lone Ranger.'

'The what?'

'Not a what, a who. He knows all about the dead, the—'

'Faith Gallagher is dead?' Bradley asked quickly, concern showing.

'Do you know this lady, Will?' Mitchell asked sincerely, lighting another cigarette.

'I told you, she was part of an old case,' Will responded, knowing he would have to defeat the bad old memories if he was to ever face her again.

'The dead, the deprived, the disappeared and the many. I only keep tabs on the happening celebrities,' Mitchell finished, aware that Bradley was lost in some kind of emotional storm, but for now was content to find his own way out.

'And how much is my visit with Tonto going to cost me?'

'Don't go calling him names. He says he's a sidekick to no man. This one shouldn't be too expensive. It's nothing special. I mean, if you wanted to see Elvis, something like that; that would cost you.'

'Mitchell, I don't know how to break this to you, but Elvis is dead.'

'No way, man,' Ford rebuked, astounded by the notion. 'He's farming melon out Idaho way. Everybody connected knows that.'

Will shook his head. 'Sometimes I worry for you, Mitchell. Forget Hi-Yo Silver. Where can I find Lo Goldman?'

Ford checked a small book and gave Bradley her office address and telephone number, then held his arm. 'If you need to talk about this, give me a call. I'm here for you, buddy.'

Bradley nodded and turned away. He wondered about Ford's choice of words. Not want to talk, but need . . . When the nightmares were choking him in his sleep again, and he couldn't close his eyes without seeing the terrifying images branded on the back of his eyelids. Without seeing her face, the helpless tears. The pain he had caused . . .

Briefly he prayed that it wouldn't come to that. But he knew that the demons of his past had woken from their slumber, and were already stalking the corridors of his consciousness, seeking him with sharp talons raised, viciously ripping every hiding place apart.

Beneath The Stars

'Where are we, Albert?' Faith asked.

It was late evening and they had walked for about an hour, straight out into the desert that surrounded her home. For the past few minutes they had been struggling up a slightly rocky incline, Faith holding his hand tight.

'About two miles from your place,' he informed her. 'From here I can see right across the desert, over your house, all the way to town – just a few lights on the horizon, speckles, like glittering dust. A tiny diamond field.'

He described it so beautifully. 'Do you come up here often?' she asked.

'All the time. I come to your place so frequently, I realised you hadn't ever visited me at my home.' Albert paused reflectively. 'Here.'

'Albert?' She grinned. 'We're in the middle of a desert. I thought you had a trailer.'

'No. I told you that because I didn't want you to think I was weird. It's great, isn't it? So tranquil. Untouched,' he marvelled. 'When my mother and father died, I just kind of checked out of society for a while. Remember the day we met?'

Faith laughed. 'You almost ran me down, hurtling along on that Doomsday device of yours. And you seriously expect me to ride pillion on that thing with you?'

'One day,' he nodded. 'People said I was nuts, coming out here for days, disappearing into the desert. But I found some caves. I met you. Your friendship helped me a lot back then. I was mixed up and didn't know how to deal with some things.'

'But this is the middle of the desert,' she repeated gently. 'You can't live here.'

31

'You do,' Albert argued.

Hiding from the world, Faith thought. 'But not in a cave like some hermit. You're too young for this, Albert.' After a second she whispered, 'I'm sorry. I know you went through a lot back then. I didn't mean—'

'I know,' he told her, gave her a brief hug. 'I like my own private space. Most nights it's warm enough to sleep under the stars. It's so romantic. On a clear night you're surrounded by the heavens, within them. Chosen . . .'

'You're very lucky, Albert,' Faith said, sharing his awe even though she could not see, experiencing the atmosphere his tones had created. 'To have found a place like this, so close to your heart.'

'I am,' he agreed solemnly, remembering his parents with misty eyes and then blinking the tears away. 'Come on. I'll take you home.'

'Not yet. You brought me up here – I want to experience everything. What's next? Where's this cave of yours?'

'Just over the ridge. It's quite a climb,' Albert advised, 'but I think I've got a couple of spare six-packs up there.'

'Good,' she said eagerly, gripping his hand once more. 'Let's go get wasted.'

DP3

Nadine Sherman struggled through the almost waist-high grass, the muddy ground absorbing her heavy work boots, trying to suck her down. The torch in her hand provided pale light in the night, and she strained to see as she searched for Drain Pipe Three.

She hated being the only woman in an all-male work environment, and was sure her fellow employees resented her intrusion upon their manly domain of radio broadcast ballgames and pin-up calendars.

She wondered how her friend Sheriff Louise Nash handled her department, fully aware – as Louise was often reminded by her people – that the decision to give her the job was not a local crowd-pleaser in Cradle. Particularly with the male deputies, who had argued that their candidate James Kennedy should have moved up from within their ranks. There had been threats of a walk-out, Louise had told her. But nothing so drastic had happened yet.

Nadine didn't know what Louise had to handle on a daily basis – her friend had been Sheriff for less than a month – but she, Nadine, had to put up with varying degrees of sexism, ranging from simple nudge-nudge name-calling to practical jokes. Most of this she could tolerate, but often her supervisors would join in the childish fun; they would laugh and tease to such an extent that if she ever felt like complaining, she was sure they would not take her seriously. Everything would be brushed under a rug and she would probably be run out of the job.

Furthermore, when any rotten work came down the line – like wading through sludge in the dead of night to check what was blocking Drain Pipe Three – she invariably pulled the short straw. In fact, the straw was usually drawn before she had a chance to see the lot, leaving her with only one option. Follow the order. Either that, or leave a job she badly needed, if only for the money so that she could feed her children: Stanley and the eponymous Baby-Poo – so nicknamed because that was what she did, often, and in the most unlikely of places. Up the walls, on her mother's bed – never inside her own crib – just to one side of the potty, never hitting the elusive target Nadine had painted on the bottom of it. In the video cabinet. In her make-up box!

She finally broke through the long grass and felt the heavy mud give way to a thick sludge. She shone the torch on the dark surface of the lake, which looked just as miserable in happy daylight.

Nadine, yawning, began to move down to the pipe, the edge of which she could see about twenty metres away, just poking over the water from the side of the low hill.

She sighed. She could remember a time when this had been Lover's Lake. She had been here in the arms of many men in the past. Her final visit here had been with the bag of puke who had given her a gorgeous, if stinky daughter and a pain-in-the-ass son who sometimes resembled his father a little too much. Then her husband had run off a year ago to date a cheerleader half his age.

'Bastard,' she whispered, almost half-heartedly, her anger and bitterness tired and worn. She grabbed the walkie-talkie from her hip. 'OK, boys, I'm at the entrance.' She shone the torch inside. Wispy cobwebs danced in the light and she shivered. 'I can't see anything.'

The tunnel was quite wide. If she had come down from the industrial plant, following toxic waste into the pipe and down to the fan that was blocked, she would have had to crawl down a long, narrow funnel. It was only on this side of the fan that DP3 could be walked down.

Nadine covered her mouth and nose, trying not to breathe in the sweating air. A rat – a large, ugly critter – stared at her through beady eyes. Instead of scurrying away it stood boldly, guarding the entrance to its lair.

'You know the procedure,' a voice came back, and she was sure she could hear the men sniggering.

34

Yes, she thought, I know the procedure. But I ain't going in there. *It stinks.* And Williard here is on look-out duty, ready to warn all his rodent buddies of my infringement on their space. What if he bites me? I could get a horrible disease and die. Do rats carry rabies? And what's lurking in the depths of the dark territory, back in the shadows where the torch has yet to penetrate?

'I don't want to go in there,' she argued, her voice sounding regrettably weak. She wished she could tell them where they could shove DP3, but the maternal part of her mind chimed up in protest: *Nadine, honey. The money you earn here might mean Baby-Poo gets a shot at college and doesn't end up doing something similar.*

Let her, she responded. She deserves it for shitting on all my best outfits.

'Go inside,' the voice instructed. They were definitely laughing at that one. 'See what the blockage is; try to remove it *man*-ually.'

'Funny, ha-ha,' she said, deciding that a lot of the males in Cradle were backward. Their attitudes, anyway.

She hesitated, taking the time to tie a clean handkerchief about her mouth and nose, and then took her first step inside.

Her legs were already covered in mud from the walk out here, but this stuff was worse. It might not be toxic, was probably harmless, but its stench overpowered her even more than the exotic aroma of Baby-Poo's offerings. At least she was wearing her gloves. If she did slip, the crap wouldn't get on her hands. She hoped.

Williard had still not moved. He chunnered, stared up at her. Thin, round eyes glinting as the moon scudded from behind the clouds. Tiny teeth chattering quickly.

This area had once been so nice, Nadine reflected, staggering forward, almost falling but catching herself on the wet, curved wall; beautiful even. But then came Circle of Life, a saving grace for the dying town of Cradle, bringing employment and profit but also destroying its tranquillity, putting columns of thick, pluming smoke on the horizon.

Circle of Life was a development plant for new, ecologically-sound washing powders and detergents. However, through their tests and research, common opinion in Cradle was that they were destroying the environment.

Nadine stepped over the rat, which had still not moved away; her boots stuck in the silt that now covered the bottom of the pipe beneath the shallow, tepid water. The stench was choking her and she considered turning back, but there was water here, which meant the crap that Circle of Life were dispensing into the environment had been partly broken down. Therefore, the block had to be up near the fan and filter.

After this she would show the guys at the main building which of the sexes had true predatory instincts. She needed a good time, and would get any man, or woman, she wanted to provide her with all the trimmings her heart – and, more importantly, her body – desired.

She swallowed deeply, trying to block out the putrid odour, and wondered what it would be like to be trapped here. She shivered at the thought, felt a cold snake coil down her spine, and wrap itself around her waist. She clamped down on her imagination before it got away from her and she ran screaming from Drain Pipe Three. That would give them all a good chuckle at her expense.

She walked deeper into the tunnel.

'I think I see the problem,' she said into the radio, observing a large bundle of rags, clothes perhaps, at the base of the hard, wire-mesh gate which protected unwitting vagrants and idiot teenagers from losing a limb in the heavy steel fans and filters. They were set on a timer and were currently still. If they had been operating, the lumbering sound would have drowned out her voice. 'I should be able to handle it.'

On the other side was the narrow pipe she would have had to crawl down if the blockage had been on the other side of the fan; it was coated in thick slime.

The torchlight flickered several times as she walked closer. She could make out a pair of blue jeans, caked in crap from the pipe, a baseball cap, a dirty sweater and . . . a pair of shoes. The pale light began to slowly fade – *not the batteries*, she thought urgently – and, the pipe giving way to the night, she felt a freezing breath on the nape of her neck, heard the rustling whisper of her name.

Startled, she spun around. There was nobody there. Just the wind, that's all, she told herself. Now, get the job done and get out of here before your imagination gives you a heart attack.

Nadine smacked the torch onto the side of the pipe and was thankful when it came on brighter than ever before.

Williard was crawling down the tunnel towards her . . . coming for her.

Tough as she was, she wished she was in the arms of a lover. Even better, that they were together somewhere romantic; and if that was not possible, then somewhere seedy with lots of kinky sex aids to try out on each other.

Even give me Baby-Poo before this, she decided desperately.

She turned, intending to grab the clothes and leave, drag them out of the tunnel so they could not clog the system again. But as she bent to take hold of the jeans she felt, with daunting horror, something inside the material. She jerked her hand away, panicking.

'Get it together, girl.'

The light began to fade again.

'No, please,' she whispered.

The pipe was now only decorated by the shallow moonlight that crept up the disgusting surface from the entrance, and fell down the clearance tunnel – a narrow, laddered pipe which led up to the hill surface. It was a rain-hole, so that any wet weather could help break the waste down and cause a run-off into Lover's Lake.

It was just your imagination, her mind said uncertainly. Nothing human would come down here. Not even a bum looking to sleep a bad night off. Just pick up the stuff and get out of here.

'Yeah,' she whispered to herself, still hesitating. Some kid just went skinny-dipping with a ladyfriend, that's all. In the excitement, he forgot his clothes at the end of the night.

'That's pretty fucking thin. Skinny-dipping in the crystal waters of the tasty-looking Lover's Lake,' she told herself sardonically, managing half a smile. 'Do the dirty. Get it over with and get out of here.'

She looked up at the silver moon at the top of the rain-hole and then slowly reached out and touched the sweater. There was a mass underneath the clothes . . . *inside them.*

She tugged at the clothes and a body rolled over. She saw his face, riddled with acne and blood, and then the rat that was nibbling at the teenager's lolling tongue.

Nadine screamed and dropped the useless torch, scampering out of the pipe as quickly as she could, vomiting twice before she splashed into the polluted lake.

Journalising

'Next time,' Faith grinned, leaning on the porch when they had returned, and hiccuping, 'we should go up on your bike.'

'Don't forget you're scared of riding it,' Albert reminded her, helping her up the few steps. 'You call it my Doomsday machine. My death-dealing device.'

'It's easy not to be afraid when you can't think straight,' she giggled. 'Uh oh – I had too much to drink.'

'No way,' Albert told her, leaving her at the door to climb onto his bike. He revved the engine. 'There's always room for a six-pack or several.'

'I had a good night, Albert. Thank you for that. Now drive safely and don't fall off.'

'Be seeing you, Faith,' Albert shouted, roaring away.

Faith smiled, waving, not minding the slip. It must be difficult for people sometimes, and Albert always meant well. He was only a kid, but so mature for his age, so responsible. He was a good friend, and now he was gone, the sound of the engine a quiet hum before it was lost to the night, the slowly falling rain and the howling winds that sounded like a wild animal baying to a moon she could not see; all heralding an unusual wet spell.

Faith entered her home, blissfully aware that she had enjoyed the night, and not once considered her malediction, the dreadful visions that had returned.

She was greeted by her answering machine.

There is one new message.

Faith sighed and collapsed onto the couch. For all its simplicity – chatting and getting drunk – the night had been one of the best times in her life for a long while. The desert walk had been gorgeous and she made a mental note to thank Albert for that the next day, when she was sober and sincere and he would believe that it was not just the Budweiser talking.

She lay back and closed her eyes, alone once more. She began to cry, tears prying an escape through her eyelids. The curse had made her a recluse, and now it was impossible to break the mould in which she had entrapped herself. Albert didn't realise what a lifeline he was – without him, his human contact, she would probably go insane.

She shook her head.

I can break the mould whenever I want, she thought. I am not a prisoner here. This is my choosing. My call. I can leave anytime I like, she concluded, without conviction.

She sat upright suddenly, swinging her legs off the sofa.

'Rewind and play,' she stated firmly.

The tape whirred, clicked, and then hummed quietly as the message was played back.

This is Lo, Faith. Pick up if you're screening . . . OK, I guess you are out, unless you just don't want to talk to me. Here's the thing: a guy was out here asking questions about you. Well, one question actually. He wants to know where you are. I told him to take a hike, but he insisted I take his name. Will Bradley. Says he's some kind of ex-cop. He might have been a hunk once, but he looks like he spent a few years too long sitting on a beach, drinking beer. Call me.

Faith swallowed deeply, sober instantly.

She had done her best not to think about Will Bradley for so long, and now he was searching for her, seeking her out, bringing all the horror back . . . And the love they had lost, stolen from them in a single night.

'We were going to be so good together,' she grieved, listening to the silence of the house, to voices drifting from the past . . .

You lovebirds get inside before the storm breaks.

But the storm had already broken, Faith reflected now. Thrashing through rancorous clouds, thundering into their lives, following them to the Radford & Doyle Institute in the embodiment of a man . . . A man with eyes that captured the light of day, absorbed it, never let it free. A man with a soul that petrified anything it touched, left it dead and rotting to waste away in the winds. A cold, dark man with the cold, dark ways of a violent storm.

Faith closed her eyes, trying to remember that terrible night, after all the years of trying to forget. She had lost so much, almost her own life. A recently formed bond had been shattered, the pieces of it scattered . . . gone. Vanished without a trace.

'Will,' she whispered, thinking of him.

I've kissed a few girls in my time. But I've never been in love.

We had so much, Faith thought, contemplating the telephone. A single call to Lo Goldman would bring the only man she had ever loved back into her life.

Never?

She smiled sweetly, remembering a conversation that might have brought about the consummation of their uncertain relationship, but instead heralded the end, like a mourning bell tolling in the night.

Until now.

It made her happy to remember him. It had not been his fault. Sure, they might have been more cautious, kept up their guard for a while longer. But Dominick Rain had fooled them all. Everybody thought he was dead. It wasn't Will's fault, she reassured herself. And now Rain was rotting in a jail cell, where he would reside until he saw his last dawn.

The killer was out of their lives for ever. It had all been a long time ago and years had been wasted. They had suffered enough and it was time to finally, truly, put it behind them and get on with living.

'We were going to be so good together,' she repeated quietly, then moved to her monitor and keyboard.

She typed for a short while, organising her thoughts.

The process was called 'journalising'; an actual recognised procedure, whereby she emptied all the conflicting opinions out of her head because they continually ricocheted off each other without strong coherence, and onto 'paper'. Once she had distanced herself from the arguments she could look at them with a cold eye, as an outsider. Objectively.

And now it seemed obvious what she had to do.

'We are going to be so good together,' she whispered, reading the words with her finger, certain in the change of tense. 'We came so close and now we have a second chance.'

Perhaps the curse she frequently complained of was finally bringing light into her life, telling her to rejoice, for there was about to be a new beginning, a second sweethearts' dance . . .

Faith stood quickly, her heart pounding as she remembered to file the entry into her journal. She moved to the telephone and called Lo at home because of the late hour.

The Wait

In a cheap room somewhere between the City of Angels and the City of Sin – Mike Castle's private name for Las Vegas; a vampiric city he was addicted to visiting, one that was sucking money from his wallet like a creature of the night taking blood from a fresh, fallen corpse – the reporter waited for the woman he craved to arrive . . . and for the men he hoped never would. Those who searched for him with the intention of breaking bones if they ever caught him. He had Vegas to thank for that, too.

But *she* should have been here by now, Mike thought, pacing the room. Should have been here hours ago. He glanced at the telephone, wondering if he should call her. But what would he say if her husband answered? Fuck him. He would tell the wife-beating sonofabitch what he thought. Madeline was leaving the bastard, anyway, so what could it hurt?

Mike grabbed the receiver and punched in her number. He let it ring once and then quickly put it down. It was crazy calling her like that. What if she hadn't left him yet, had decided to go when he was at work to avoid a confrontation? Or when he was with one of his mistresses?

Inside, he knew that Madeline was not that kind of person. She would want to sever all ties she had with him, look him in the eyes and tell him that she was never coming back. And that he was not to bother looking for her.

Perhaps she was just held up in traffic, he countered, not very convincingly. Stuck in traffic on a deserted stretch of highway. Yeah, right.

He would give her until morning.

He grinned humourlessly; there was the possibility that she had come to her senses and realised that life with a sleazy reporter who missed more deadlines than he hit was not worth the loss of the wealth that she had at the moment. Even if that wealth did have a terrible price. Personally, he was hoping she would bring a little hard cash along with her so that he could settle a few old gambling debts and keep his body intact.

Mike sat down on the edge of the bed.

This was the rendezvous point; tonight was the night. Madeline would be here, even if she was a little late . . .

He needed that money. She'd better show.

He closed his eyes. God, he wanted her, couldn't wait to hold her in his arms again. He yearned for her gorgeous body to be on top of his once more. For Mike, the relationship was purely physical, and parasitical.

It had been a long time since Castle had been in a steady relationship with a woman. Not that there had been any men. Just a lot of one-night stands and easy sex.

Mike knew men and women in his circle of friends who were having affairs – editors carrying on secret liaisons with young trainee reporters, columnists who kept scorecards with their opposite numbers on other papers, any number of flings between people in book publishing. He enjoyed being numbered among them. Free.

With Madeline there had been no pretence. They had great sex and she was very rich, might even help him out of a tight spot with several different loansharks. The money probably had the edge in his priorities.

He recalled what Madeline had told him at their last meeting here.

I want to leave him, Mike. I want to be with you.

He could easily live with her wanting to be with him, but this sudden talk one night of her leaving her husband had made him shy away slightly. He didn't want to get tied down to one woman, unless it was a bondage game . . . But Madeline was so good to him. Together they performed pleasurable acts he had only imagined until now. To resist her would be to deny his body a great prize. Besides, he could always cheat on her if he ever got bored.

Mike Castle was a rancid sexist who only knew how to use

women, and had no respect for them. He would cheerfully admit this in any bar for the cost of a drink. He was slime.

The sun rising, temperatures soaring, they had made love the following morning. It was soft and slow, gentle, but disciplined and perfect. The kind of love familiarity and intimate knowledge breed.

Then they had moved to the deserted motel pool, held hands like teenagers sweet on each other after making out for the first time. It was there that he fearfully realised he might be falling for her. He ignored his beating heart, and reassured himself that he was in the game only for the money.

Do you know what I love about you the most, Mike Castle? You have such a tender touch . . . so unlike his.

They made daring love in the pool, ignoring the threat of discovery as he realised that this would either be a new beginning and an end to all his financial problems, or the conclusion of their relationship. When they climbed out of the water, Madeline told him to be here in a week.

She had returned to their room, dressed and then walked to her car. She blew him a kiss as she drove away, wheels kicking dust into the air, and that was the last time he had seen her.

Where was she?

The night was long, time stretching to infinity. His right leg was troubling him, the joints aching from an old injury inflicted in a car crash. He had come to trust the unexpected bouts of pain as a bad omen, but he ignored its warning this time, swallowing a couple of Jericho painkillers.

It was unlikely that she would have decided to stay with her husband.

On the day they had met, Madeline had been wearing large sunglasses, despite the grey clouds, and heavy make-up. He knew what that meant: back in the old days when he was a real journalist, he'd interviewed and written about guys on several construction crews who had spoken proudly about the control they exerted on their women to keep them in line, about long skirts or trousers on particularly hot days, about wearing sweaters or tops with sleeves during sweltering heat. About excessive make-up that hid ugly bruising.

Once their passionate intimacy had grown to a greater trust and understanding, Madeline had told him about the beatings, and how when she made love to her husband she wondered if that was how it felt to be raped because he was so violent and dominant. She no longer desired him, but was afraid to leave.

That was when they had first talked about a life together, joking and laughing because, at first, they had both doubted it would ever happen. Castle especially.

But now the truth of the moment was upon them.

Mike believed he was finally close to crawling from under the weight of his debts, and even if he didn't intend remaining with Madeline for ever, he had at least given her the impetus to leave her husband.

He lay on the bed, thinking of a stranger he had never met hitting the woman he . . . Almost said it, he thought. He didn't love Madeline. He cared for her deeply and she was great in bed. He cared a lot for her money. That wasn't love; it was the burning heart of lust. But what if Russell Crowe could never understand it was over, that his wife had left for good? What would he do to keep her?

The Big Wheel – Two

Faith sat bolt upright in her chair, knocking an empty glass from the wooden arm. She gasped as it shattered on the polished floor. She would clean it up, but make sure she didn't walk barefoot until Albert had checked for any missed shards the next morning.

There was a song playing on the radio, but she didn't recognise the tune; the music was classical, quiet. It must have lulled her into a doze.

'Time?' she asked, rubbing her face.

Eleven thirty-three, an electronic voice informed her as she stood and crossed the spacious room.

At the window she listened to the rain pattering onto the glass. It was a good downpour, but not the storm everyone was predicting. She wished she could see the wind blowing, and not just hear its angry howl.

'Curtains close,' she said, and heard them *swish* across the tracks as they closed.

The curse had paid for all this – benefits that most blind people could not even imagine; voice-commanded modules which afforded her a host of luxuries. All she needed now was a robot to do the house-cleaning and she would be happy.

Of course, for that she had Albert. He comes out here so often, she thought, and I know so little about him. I have cut myself off from society so well that I don't even have friends. This is not living! She decided to make a conscious effort to discover new things about Albert, perhaps even go into town – something she had not done for over a year.

The last time she was in Cradle, a gentleman had guided her across the street and she had felt a piercing pain in her chest, like a pin slowly rupturing a balloon. In less than a week the man had died from a heart attack, and she had known it was going to happen. That was one of the reasons she rarely strayed from her home. What else was out there?

People would wonder who she was. They probably gossiped about the blind hermit who lived out in the desert on her own, the children spooked by the weird woman who didn't like company.

She had lost so much; even though she had known so little when she had lost her sight. Just a child, barely out of diapers.

'Radio off,' she said severely, old emotions rising up like the dead to haunt her. Damn the curse, she thought.

She heard a volley of thunder in the distance.

And then silence. Except for the heart of the gathering storm.

It was generally believed that if you lost one of your senses, the ones remaining attained heightened levels not achieved by other people.

Normal people.

Give me a break, she thought, shutting her angry psyche down. I don't want to be in a sulking mood tonight. She thought about the reason she had been startled awake, sitting before her computer . . .

I can hear a truck rumbling in the darkness, even though . . .

Faith stopped typing in the shadows and listened to the night, the sound she was describing. There was no truck. And if there was, she wouldn't be able to hear it, she thought. The highway was too far away.

It was the curse, poisoning her mind.

The Big Wheel is from a truck. It is speeding through the night, hammering the highway.

The driver is a burly man, with a spider-web tattoo on one bicep and . . . But my mind passes him by. It is a camera drifting about the front of the cab and I can only see what it shows me. Tiny plastic animals are mounted on spring bases and fixed to the dash. They wobble and bounce into each other. Behind his tattooed shoulder is a poster of a woman clad only in sexy underwear. It is not a model, but a blown-up picture of his girl . . .

48

The camera has moved around the side of the truck now. It is long and dirty and white.

A logo and the name of the company are in fancy lettering – a distinctive pattern. I cannot make out what they say or mean.

This I know to be important. It is a mystery. There is always a mystery, a puzzle to be solved – nothing is ever what it seems. I try to pull the camera of my mind back. It is too close to the side of the charging vehicle – the writing a blur. The camera refuses to budge.

Frustrated with the fight, I let it drift down to the spinning wheel.

The truck is gone.

The Big Wheel keeps on turning.

I break the connection.

Damn this affliction, Faith thought again.

If only she could see. She could sketch the logo, the elaborate lettering. It was obviously the name of some kind of company, but why had the malediction deprived her of it?

Live life to the full, she mused. So instead of sending her mind to a blockaded part of her sanity until the new visions stopped, she welcomed them with open arms and was determined to seek out the truth of what they meant.

Maybe even save some lives, she thought, and tried not to think about Denver, Detective Bradley and the Bad Things that had happened. She missed the police detective, wished she could think of him without the association of Dominick Rain.

Maybe even save lives . . . *including my own . . .*

Soul-Mates

'Nadine,' Sheriff Louise Nash said gently, placing a soft hand on her friend's arm. 'How are you holding up?'

'Well, my stomach has finally finished throwing up the meals of the day,' Nadine explained, still trembling slightly. 'I guess I'm doing OK for a girl who has just seen her first dead body. That's if you don't count her ex-husband.' Nadine tried to smile, but it looked grim and wrong. 'I could never find a pulse, anyway.'

Louise clutched her arm sympathetically. They had been buddies since childhood – the day they were born, in fact – only the wall of a delivery room and split seconds separating their arrival into the big, bad world. 'Soul-mates for ever' was a comment made by one of the nurses, her mother had told Louise years later. The nurse had been right, Louise reflected. Always there for each other. Never apart. She had been a bastion of emotional support during Nadine's bitter divorce.

It was Louise's first dead body, too – at least as the Sheriff of Cradle. As a deputy she had seen several others; all heart attacks or accidental deaths, without evidence of foul play simply because there was none.

She looked at all the deputies she had called out working under the floodlights they had set up at the edge of Lover's Lake. Visibility was still not perfect, but it was better than the darkness that lurked at their pale light's perimeter. She had only held the position of Sheriff for a short time, and many members of the department – through their support of Deputy James Kennedy – had disagreed with her appointment. If this incident at DP3 turned out to be nothing more than a dopehead falling down a hole, it would provide them with yet more ammunition against her.

50

She looked at her friend. At least Nadine had managed to keep her humour and wits about her, and had not given way to shock.

'What are you doing out here, Nadine?' Louise asked suddenly, watching a couple of deputies inspecting the rim of Drain Pipe Three. Inside the tunnel, and on the field above where a narrow hole allowed rainfall into the system, thus creating a greater run-off and helping to dilute the seepage, were Cradle's three forensics experts, working the scene with customary proficiency.

She saw James Kennedy march out of the pipe and glance at her angrily. She turned away.

'There was some kind of block in the pipe, near the fan. I went down to—'

'I know,' Louise said, and then took the hard edge out of her voice. 'I mean, what are *you* doing working in a stinkhole like this?'

'I have to feed my children, you know? My life hasn't been all wine and roses since . . .' Nadine sniffed, couldn't prevent the tears. 'I miss him, Louise. I know Jimmy was a good-for-nothing drunken bastard, but I miss him.'

'No. Don't ever say that. He was scum and good riddance to him. You just miss there being a man around the house, that's all.'

Louise hugged her friend, who stood tall and lifted her head. The tears stopped quickly.

'You're right. Better not let the guys see me now.' Nadine grinned mirthlessly. 'They think I'm a tough-as-nails hard-assed bitch. They don't know the amount of times I go home, put the kids to bed and then just lie in a hot tub . . . crying. God, I'm sorry, Louise. You don't need this now.'

'It's easy,' Louise assured her. 'Soul-mates to the end, remember?'

'Always,' Nadine replied, genuinely smiling.

'Good. I'm going to have a car take you home. I'll check on you tomorrow.'

'Hey!' Deputy Kennedy called from DP3. Various members of the crew looked around, and Louise was certain that those within the pipe had also stopped work to listen. 'When you ladies have finished exchanging recipes, we got some work to do here!'

51

* * *

Deputy James Kennedy was a handsome man, in a pin-up calendar kind of way. He was well built and well groomed, obviously spending as much time in front of a mirror as he did in the gym, as he did on the job. His mother had wanted to name him after the assassinated President, but his father had won a compromise, settling for a 'J' initial.

Louise approached him at the entrance of Drain Pipe Three, sighing audibly. Kenny was good-looking, and good in bed, too. It was a shame that he had the male chauvinistic attitudes of an intellectually challenged Neanderthal. The day she had discovered these truths was the last day he'd slept in her bed; the day she'd been promoted over him was the last day of a volatile yet tolerable friendship.

They were alone at the edge of the tunnel.

'You spoke to me once too often like that in the bedroom and I kicked you out,' she reminded him in low tones. 'You shout at me like that again in front of these people and I'll personally sign transfer papers for you.'

'Is that a threat, Lou?' he spat, leaning close.

She hated it when he called her that. A few of the guys – most of them, she thought miserably – used the name to remind her of how wrong they thought her posting was; that the job should have been given to a man. Namely Deputy James Kennedy: college football hero and local boy made good.

There were other people who couldn't make up their minds and were sitting on the fence, simply wanting to get on with their job and their lives. Not wanting to support anybody, or knowing who to support. To them she was Sheriff Nash.

Now and again somebody would dare to call her Louise in front of their peers. She didn't understand why it was such a big problem to address her as Sheriff Nash, and why so many people couldn't get past it.

'Take it how you like, Kenny,' she told him, wondering fleetingly where the good times had gone, then deciding that all the good times had been between the sheets; other than that they had argued a lot. 'I was consoling a shocked witness, and your behaviour hasn't exactly conformed to a professional standard recently.'

'You got us all out of bed for this?' Kenny asked, shaking his head. He began to walk away. Louise thought about ignoring him, but was aware of the listening ears scattered about the scene. If she let him go, it would count against her. It was a stupid game that compromised all their work. She jogged to catch up. 'It's just some kid,' Kenny continued, knowing that she had no option but to follow. Score one for him. 'Probably drugged out, and he fell down the rain-hole. For this, you wake up the whole department.'

'I've been on the job for less than a month, Kenny. I need all the bases covered – I don't want to miss anything. Your support would be nice. If not, your silence. Why does this have to be so personal for you?'

'Because it is,' he sneered quietly. 'You got my promotion. You're enjoying the power, aren't you?' Then he added loudly: 'You always did like it on top.'

Louise felt her cheeks blushing, not wanting the whole world to know her sexual preferences. 'Let's discuss this matter another time, Kenny. OK?'

'*Sheriff Nash!*'

She turned and looked up. In the field above, on the hill, was Wade Phelan, head of the small forensics unit. His long blond hair seemed to shimmer in the moonlight.

'What is it?' she asked.

'You best come up here. We got something.'

Louise shrugged at Kenny, and then began to climb the hill.

The Scarred Man

To Jenny Klein the man with the scarred face seemed like just another john. He paid her up front – that was the only way Jenny would work; she had been stiffed once or twice by some of the sick bastards who demanded services way beyond the call of duty, so now she demanded what she called a retaining fee before she moved off the Boulevard – and then she walked with the man across the same stars Will Bradley had wandered down that same morning, towards her apartment.

'I really, if you don't mind, I—' the man stammered.

'Hey, cutie, what's wrong?' Jenny asked. She was a nice person. Some of her friends in the business said she was too nice, that one day it was going to get her seriously hurt. Not tonight, she thought. This guy was acting like he'd never even been with a woman before. She held his hand softly. 'Why are you all nervous?'

'I'm hungry,' Dominick Rain whispered strangely.

'Well, if you like we can just sit down and have a coffee, maybe a burger or two,' she told him, and they stopped and faced each other. 'It's your money. But I know something a lot sweeter I'll let you taste.' She stepped close to him and manoeuvred her hand up the inside of his jeans leg. She felt his erection and giggled. 'My, you *are* hungry,' she grinned.

'It's been a long time for me,' he told her. 'I want this to be special.'

'I have a room. It's got a bed and everything,' she boasted. 'Come on.'

He hesitated, so she took his hand and led the way as she would in a short while. This was going to be easy money. He might even be a virgin. Once in a while she enjoyed her work, found the right man. Like now. A virgin, maybe. She laughed.

'What's so funny?' he asked, sounding almost paranoid.

They crossed the busy night streets.

'We're gonna have a good time, baby!'

It had to be clean, Dominick thought. It always had to be clean. That had been drilled into him as a child.

The sheets on the bed were tidy and pressed, the carpet recently vacuumed. He moved into the bathroom.

Jenny sat on the bed. Her client wasn't Richard Gere and things like *Pretty Woman* just didn't happen in real life. Not in her life, anyway. But at least he appeared to be a nice guy; she had been around long enough to know that there were too few of those about.

She began to unbutton her blouse, and patted the bed. 'Come sit down,' she told him.

'In a minute,' he said, finishing his inspection of the walls and the tub. He checked the toilet seat, and was disappointed to find a fine layer of grime on the underside. He sighed deeply, torn between his obsession and his dark desires.

All the towels were laid out correctly, except for one which was rucked slightly. He smoothed it out.

'What's your name?' Jenny called. Obviously this was not going to be a quick one. And in cases like that, she'd rather take her time, too. Enjoy the company. 'What are you doing in there?'

Dominick stared at his reflection in the mirror, studying his face. When he was younger he had been quite handsome, but in prison some roughnecks had taken a fancy to his pretty boy looks. When he put up a struggle because he didn't want to be their 'girl', they had seriously scarred his face, destroying his features.

'Dominick,' he responded, running the faucet in the bathtub, washing away a few hairs that were caught in the plughole. It could have been a lot worse. The bedroom, where he would perform, was clean.

When he returned a moment later she was lying on the bed in her underwear. She had dropped her clothes carelessly onto the floor.

'No,' he whispered, bending to pick them up. He found a hanger in a wardrobe for her dress and fastidiously put it in place.

'You paid me for the privilege of cleaning my apartment?' she joked. 'Why not look at me instead.'

He stopped, about to straighten her shoes, and glanced over his shoulder. She was beautiful, her body slender. There was only one thing wrong with Jenny, and he would soon fix that.

'I know you're hungry, so why are you torturing yourself like this? If you're a little shy, don't worry. I won't bite. Unless, of course, you want me to. Come here,' she told him, holding out her hand, her nails painted the colour of blood.

He stepped towards the bed and then moved back to the shoes. 'Come on, baby,' she encouraged.

Before moving to the bed he tidied the stilettos. One had fallen to the floor on its side, and they were the wrong way round. He put the left shoe to the left.

Finally, satisfied that everything was in order, Dominick approached her. He reached into the pocket of his jeans and slowly revealed a black bandanna. 'Will you wear this – over your eyes? Please?'

So that was why he was all nervous. He'd probably been with plenty of women, but each time had trouble expressing whatever kinky desires he had in mind. Wearing a blindfold wasn't too much to ask, she decided.

'I guess you have your own special appetite,' she purred, scampering across the bed eagerly. 'It's going to cost you a little extra, though.'

He nodded, unfolded a hundred from his pocket and placed it on her dresser, a shambles of cheap jewellery and perfumes. He resisted the urge to organise them.

'Tie it for me,' she told him quickly, before he could be distracted by the jumble. She turned and leaned her head back, revealing a soft neck, skin of silk.

His touch was gentle, although she felt him tug at the bandanna a little too tightly. There was a knot of pleasurable tension in her stomach as he told her to lie on her back. She obeyed him, blind, listening to the sounds as he undressed. Then she realised how little she knew of what was happening around her, how vulnerable a person is without the sense of sight. How much could go wrong . . .

Suddenly she didn't welcome the darkness.

'Let's play a game,' he told her.

'What are you doing?' Jenny asked, aware that one of her stockings was torn, the nylon peeling apart.

'How do you feel?' Dominick responded.

She thought for a second. She was afraid, but at the same time she was excited; the mystery of what he was doing, what he could do next, arousing her. She wasn't tied, could run and flee if he tried anything too dominant. Could scream for help. Occasionally, what must be a knife edge touched her leg, but he never cut her – only her stockings. A delicate touch. Strangely, even as he performed his perverted delights, she felt safe. Sexy.

Something wet touched her breast.

His tongue, she thought. And then he was pulling impatiently at her bra.

'Easy, Dominick,' she soothed. The straps fell away. They must have been cut too. Expenses, she thought, wondering flatly what additional sums she could extract from him. If he did the same to her suspender belt and panties, this night was really going to cost him.

Suddenly, she felt ice on her nipples. She shivered, surprised. Hadn't heard him go to the freezer. Pay attention, she told her roaming mind.

'How do you feel?' he repeated.

'Scared,' she told him uncertainly. 'But also, I think this is a little fun. Nervous.'

'It was never fun for me,' he whispered harshly, suddenly angry. He pinned her to the bed with one strong hand.

'Hey!' she protested, genuinely afraid that this was no sexual game, but an encounter with a sick man, some kind of deviant who now intended to hurt her.

'Take it easy,' he whispered, trying to calm her. Perhaps this was all part of his game. She wanted to remove the blindfold, but he pinned her arms down with his strong knees and sat on her flat stomach. She tried to scream but he clamped a hand over her mouth.

'How does it feel?' he asked again, but continued before she could answer: 'You're blind, just like me. Now do you understand why I need your help? Why you have to stay down there all the time and never, ever leave me alone? Why you have to wash all the blood away?'

Jenny began to cry. He removed his hand from her mouth.

'I don't know what you're talking about. Please don't hurt me.'

'Try walking around,' he said gently, but would not let her up. 'Not easy, is it?'

'Please, don't hurt me. I'll give you your money back. You can do anything . . . but don't kill me. Please!' She struggled, the knife suddenly at her throat. 'No!' She tried to scream. 'Please, God – no . . .' Her hands were stuck at her sides, her struggles futile.

'Did you know that when blind people die, you can't see the fear in their eyes? The fading light of life.'

And then, there was no stopping the knife.

Small-Town Murder

'Wade. Bobby,' Louise said, out of breath as she approached the two men on the hill at Drain Pipe Three. There were no floodlights here, the only illumination coming from the headlights of their cars. It was a miracle they had found anything, and lucky they had found it so quickly, otherwise their batteries would be flat. 'Can we get some real light up here! Tell me something nice.'

'We don't deal in sweet dreams, Sheriff Nash, you know that,' Bobby Fullton said wryly. He was an old man with thinning hair, his back stooped slightly. Louise felt sorry for him. Six years ago his wife had drowned and ever since then Bobby always seemed so lonely and so very sad. A true smile had not graced his face in a long time. It was as though he was waiting to die, to be with her again.

Louise grinned when Wade Phelan gave him a stern look. It was in great affection, the two friends often acting like an old vaudeville routine. However, Wade did resent the fact that Bobby couldn't make up his mind about the new Sheriff. Still sitting on that fence, Phelan's glance said.

'I know,' Louise responded. 'If it's dead, you'll be there. Now, what have you got?' she asked, finishing the banter.

'Should I tell her?' the older man asked Phelan. 'Or do you want the honour?'

'You found the blood. It's your show,' Wade told him.

'Blood – where?' Louise interposed.

'Yes, my friend, I did. But you spotted the footprint, Mr Phelan.'

'What footprint?' Louise snapped. Together they could be cute, but she didn't have the patience to watch their act after her confrontation with Deputy Kennedy.

'It's not actually a footprint, Louise,' Wade told her quickly, not

59

wanting to face her wrath. 'A *shoe*print, really. And just a partial – I'd guess at about size forty-six. Guy with at least one big foot. Give me a couple of hours and I can probably give you an accurate size.'

'My turn now,' Fullton said, recovered and ready to roll again. 'Look over here,' he directed Louise, shining his torch into the rain-hole. 'You see that dark patch a couple of rungs down?'

She nodded.

'Blood,' Fullton informed her.

'But if he fell into the hole he could have cracked his head on the way down,' Louise observed.

Wade nodded. 'But the guy down the hole has teensy-weensy feet. I checked the inside of his shoe. We also found some prints on one of the top rungs. I bet you my house—'

'You don't have a house, Wade,' Louise reminded him.

'I bet my camper and Fullton's house, that the kid has a couple of broken fingers.'

'Because he was hanging on to that ladder for his life?' Louise said thoughtfully.

'Because he was pushed down that hole,' Fullton concluded. 'Murdered. Anybody for an autopsy?'

'Do it,' Louise decided.

Hard Rain

Dominick was disappointed to see that the woman he had killed was not actually blind. She had a bandanna tied about her eyes so that she could not see, but there was no way she could have been his mother. The doctors in the asylum had told him that when he was killing the blind women, he was actually re-enacting the death of his mother, over and over again.

He remembered the blindfold his parents had forced him to wear. Lorna, too.

Do you understand how I feel now? his mother had taunted.

He missed Lorna, her gentle touch, their love. He wanted to contact her, but didn't know where she was. He was jealous that she was sleeping with another man, but he knew that their special bond would never be broken, and that they would soon be together again. Always.

But for now, he only had the miserable dead for company.

It hurt him to leave the room in this red mess, but there was no time to clean it up. Somebody else could have that pleasure.

When he returned to his hotel room he found a message from Lorna. His heart quickened at the thought of her coming here, pushing the note under his door. He touched the writing. She was annoyed that he had not been here and would contact him again soon. She said it was time.

Dominick wondered how she would feel if she knew what he had done tonight. Would she ever want to see him again?

In his room he showered for over an hour under hissing hot water. He scrubbed all the blood off and then scrubbed some more, almost making himself bleed in the process.

And then he slept, dreaming of Lorna and what the message meant.

It is time.
She had located Faith Gallagher.

A Cowboy And His Horse

Mike Castle was dozing lightly when the motel door crashed in, and he realised immediately that Madeline's money might never be given the chance to save him. He tried to run for the bathroom, but somebody grabbed him and easily threw him back on the bed with strong arms.

Mike lay still, trying not to tremble. He wondered, staring into the hard eyes of his assailants, what would happen if Madeline arrived now, and he realised he cared for her less than he had originally believed. He would do anything to save his own hide, including handing Madeline to the goon squad, a trade for a few hours' headstart. Let them have their way with her. Morally reprehensible, but that was Mike all over.

The reporter recognised the men who had found him. They were Roy Rogers and Trigger – a pair of trigger-happy bastards. Roy – real name Maurice Pendleton – was a great fan of those old Westerns and his partner gladly went along with his buddy's crazy ideas. They wore jeans and Stetsons, and carried old-fashioned six-shooters on their hips, keeping the heavy artillery in the back of their automobile.

These two had caught up with Mike in San Diego, and he knew he'd been lucky then to escape with all his fingers attached to each hand.

'Watch him, Mule,' Roy instructed the much larger Trigger.

Roy began to search through Mike's travel bag and came up with a pair of jeans, a couple of clean shirts and a bottle of cheap aftershave.

'You're a hard man to find, Mikey,' Roy observed once he had finished his search.

'Lucky for me,' the journalist quipped, trying to grin but failing miserably.

'Not lucky enough,' Trigger reminded him, leering close.

'There are a lot of posses out looking for you. You owe a lot of money to a lot of different people. And I figure we could help you with your financial difficulties,' the smarter cowboy explained.

'Can I hurt him, Roy?' Trigger asked.

'Not yet,' Roy told his partner, motioning for him to take a step back. 'How much is the total figure?'

'Somewhere in the region of a hundred and fifty thousand dollars,' Castle muttered. 'But I'm real close to getting it. No shit. Clearing all my tabs. *Real close.*'

'You won't have to clear them all,' Roy informed him with a warm smile. 'We have only come to collect on behalf of Mr Giovanni the sum of sixty-seven thousand dollars, plus interest. Mr Giovanni views this as a serious matter and a personal betrayal. But, I have a business proposition for you.'

When he was growing up, Maurice Pendleton used to love those old black and white Westerns. Roy Rogers and his sequined shirts was his favourite. The guy had class, style and charisma. Then came Vietnam and a whole lot of bad shit had come down on Maurice. It was over there that his mind had splintered. All the trauma had been bottled up and left with Maurice, and it was Roy Rogers who had returned from the jungles, the heat and the horror. Riding out, into an eternal sunset.

He had found muscle work with Ramone Giovanni, and had hooked up with a retard the guys called Horse. He had given Horse a name: Trigger. An unbreakable bond was formed. Roy had the brains and would take care of them both, while Trigger had the brawn to keep them alive until they realised their dream.

Roy didn't ever want to face what Maurice had done in Vietnam, and he knew times were worse now. War was only to serve the slavering, bickering politicians. And with the proverbial depressing of a button, or the twist of a key, every man, woman and child in the world would pay for their inability to agree.

The Big Nuke Trigger had always feared would come down on them all.

So the dream was to save enough money for themselves, get

an underground shelter. Guard it with their lives until the day the world ended. And then rule the roost – whatever was left of it.

Often, sleep would only come to Trigger after Roy had sat up, describing the shelter to him. The barbed-wire perimeter fencing to keep intruders out. The landmines they would place on the property. The armoury within to protect themselves from New World marauders who had not had the foresight to prepare for The Big Nuke. They would survive and be safe . . . and happy dreams would imbue Trigger's sleep.

Roy remembered a book Maurice Pendleton had once studied, a long time ago. It was called *Of Mice and Men* by John Steinbeck, and was about simple men during hard times who worked the land and lived for a dream. It occurred to him that he and Trigger were a modern-day George and Lennie, only instead of stroking rabbits and farming alfalfa, they would tend to their weapons and prepare for the New World.

'For an even seventy thousand dollars – that's right, just seventy big ones – we'll let you live and tell Mr Giovanni that you were killed by rival collectors. Dead when we caught up with you,' Roy smiled.

Mike grinned, seeing a way out. These clowns would let him go; he'd get the money off Madeline and then dump her.

Roy knew exactly what the reporter was thinking, and joined him in a small laugh. It was a scam he and Trigger had worked before, and there was only one way it truly succeeded. Once the fugitive had paid up in full he had to be killed, otherwise word might get back to Giovanni that he was still alive.

'Do we have a deal, Mike?' Roy asked genially.

'I certainly think we do.'

Two Shoes

Wade Phelan stared at the computer as it finished constructing the three-dimensional model which it then rotated on the screen. He had been one size out when guessing the size of the partial shoeprint they had found. It was a size forty-five. The dead boy's feet were much smaller.

They had all agreed at the scene that the kid was murdered, and had begun during this long night to gather the first scraps of evidence that would prove their theories.

He contemplated throwing on his jacket and going back out to the hill to see if they had missed anything, when Fullton came in through the swinging doors.

'I've finished my preliminary checks,' he told Phelan, 'and I'm about to start slicing and dicing. You want in?'

Wade looked over Fullton's shoulder, through the double windows, into the cold sterility of the next room. The naked body of the teenager lay whitely on the table. He could see scales for weighing various removed organs, a hanging recorder to dictate details. Sharp drilling and cutting instruments.

'I'll pass on that,' he said with a shudder.

'Somebody else was up there when the kid died,' the old man stated.

'Maybe,' Wade shrugged.

It was the first murder in Wade's time in Cradle. Over a decade. The town was a peaceful haven, a loving and sharing community, racked by the occasional bit of scandal, sure, but nothing like this . . .

'It could be an old print,' he said thoughtfully, not ready to accept that the killer was residing in the community. 'Or maybe the kid was up there with a friend who got scared after the accident.'

'I can already tell you the kid died from a broken neck. Snapped the instant he hit the ground – fell on his head.' Fullton broke the pencil he was holding in his hand. It cracked in the night, a splinter of sound.

'So he died from the fall. That means —'

'He also has a couple of broken fingers, just as you predicted, Wade. And unlike the neck, they didn't just snap; they were crushed. He was pushed down the hole, and managed to hold on to the ladder before the killer mashed his fingers with a heavy shoe. Under his nails I've found some fibres that don't match the clothes he was wearing. To be honest, at the moment, I'd guess they were silk.'

Wade digested what he was being told. Silk, huh? Somebody who didn't mind getting expensive clothes dirty, or a woman. Someone who wore heavy, big shoes.

'What was the kid's name?' he asked.

He might just be a doped up teenager, Wade thought, and from the drugs they had found in his clothing that was more than likely, but he had a family. He had a life, even if he was wasting it at the time of his death. He'd had a future, the opportunity to catch up and put the wrong things right. Make amends.

But now all the chances had slipped through his fingers. He had nothing. Wade sighed. They were talking about the dead boy as though he was not a real person; Fullton was about to matter-of-factly hack him open and study his insides. This wasn't an everyday occurrence in Cradle, however many autopsies Fullton had performed in the big, bad city wilderness.

'Ricky Turner. We found his wallet. I think Sheriff Nash went to talk to his parents.'

Wade nodded sombrely. Poor Ricky Turner. He looked through the windows of the doors a final time. Then: 'I'm going back out to the scene,' he told Fullton. 'We might have missed something.'

They had to find out who did this.

Wade was surprised to discover Sheriff Louise Nash still out at DP3, standing in the fine drizzle, alone on the grassy hill near the rain-hole. He stooped under the police tape, reflected that he had never even seen it in use until this dark night, and approached her. Even in her uniform, she looked beautiful under the moon.

'Hey, sweetheart,' he whispered softly.

She spun, startled. Her eyes were misty, her cheeks wet.

'Don't cry,' Wade said quickly, hugging her, holding her. The murder had hit her hard. 'Did you speak with Ricky's parents yet?'

'I couldn't do it, Wade,' Louise cried. 'How could I wake them in the middle of the night, disturb them with this terrible news? How could I do that?'

'Come on.'

Wade held her hand gently and led her away from the scene to his car. They sat in silence. Wade let her cry on his shoulder, wishing he knew the right words to say, but coming up empty. So he let her weep.

'They should have this last night of peace,' she sobbed. 'There will be so many sleepless nights ahead, so many nightmares . . .'

Wade cuddled her, kissed her softly on the cheeks.

They had only slept together twice, both times victims to passion and circumstances rather than pre-arranged dates. Neither spoke of their feelings to the other, or other people. They were sacred and only for themselves to know. It was only now that Wade acknowledged how much he cared for her, that she wasn't just a female conquest. He let her cry, until she finally came through the other side.

He noticed the change. She moved off his shoulder, sat upright. Her posture was stronger. She quickly wiped at her eyes. He recognised that the rare display of vulnerability was over, but that he had been privileged to share it. She sniffed a final time, and then grabbed his hand firmly.

'*Was* he murdered, Wade? Have you and Fullton confirmed your theories?'

Wade nodded slowly and she closed her eyes. He told her about the fibres and the crushed fingers, the size of the shoe. When she opened her eyes he saw that they were no longer red, but bright with the desire to solve the mystery.

Come morning, Louise thought, the whole town will be looking to me as Sheriff for answers, the whole department looking for instruction. They would need leadership. She could not break down then. It was time to be strong and do the job. She acknowledged sadly that some – Deputy Kennedy, for example – would be watching for her collapse.

'Come on,' Louise said, and climbed from the car. She returned to the hole, shining a torch, careful of the print in the damp ground which they had already moulded, measured and photographed.

'Wait up, Louise,' Wade called after her, jogging over. 'He was doing drugs. I'm sure Fullton will tell us that in the morning.'

'But why kill a drug addict?'

'Maybe it was his dealer.'

'There isn't that big a drug problem in town,' Louise informed him. 'Mostly, it's just kids fooling around.'

'Then this kid must have seen something,' Wade theorised. 'The other guy must have been up here doing something illegal, or personally humiliating. It was just crappy luck that their paths happened to cross.'

'Maybe you should have the lake dredged, see what it pulls up.'

'No. I'm already a laughing stock with the department for the way I got them all out of bed earlier,' she said ruefully.

'You've got a job to do, Louise. You do it any way you see fit,' Wade assured her.

'It could have been an executive from Circle of Life getting his jollies with a lady of the night, or a gay lover, or it could be serious foul play.'

Wade nodded reluctantly. 'Go with your instincts, sweetheart. Don't let anybody tell you any different.' Under the winking stars, as they spoke unromantically of death, Wade realised he loved Louise Nash. He would do anything for her. Even die.

'One thing is for certain,' she told the man she also loved. 'Somebody in Cradle has a secret to hide. One they will kill to protect. I want that lake dredged now. If anything's down there, I want to know by sun-up.'

Day Two – 0547

Men With Men

It was the twilight of sunrise, the candescent yellow orb cresting the horizon when the two former Denver cops met at Venice Beach, Los Angeles and wandered along the boardwalk.

There was a young, loving couple playing an early game of one-on-one on the desolate basketball courts which would soon be a chaotic dance of hustlers and genuine athletes, sweltering to the heavy beat of pounding balls and lofty jump-shots. At the moment the bouncy, happy girl was teaching her boyfriend a trick or two as she completed another basket. There were also a couple of vendors setting up their market stalls and a few skaters and early morning cyclists – but mostly Will Bradley and Mitchell Ford had the beach and boardwalk to themselves.

'Did you speak with Lo Goldman yet?' Mitchell asked, already well into his first packet of smokes for the day.

'Those things will kill you,' Will observed, putting off the subject. They cut onto the beach.

'Everybody dies sooner or later,' Mitchell retorted. 'I'd rather go doing something I like – not fighting and struggling against an addiction, taking all the pleasure out of it. What did Lo tell you?'

'I contacted her yesterday, but she wasn't interested. Then she called late last night, said she had spoken with Faith and that she had an address for me near a town called Cradle. I gave my client the location. Case closed. Easiest money I've ever earned.'

'Then why did you want to talk about it?' Ford asked, stopping to sit on the sand. They looked out at the ocean, a vast world of mystery at their fingertips, he thought. An emptiness that stretched as far as he could see, one that suddenly filled his soul. The sun reflected white patches on the waves and Ford sighed.

He lit another cigarette, inhaled deeply. He felt as though he had not contributed to life in a long time.

'Because . . .' Will began, and then decided that was all he had to say.

A windsurfer trying to catch the early morning breeze fell from his board, splashing into the water. They both laughed without humour. Two troubled minds searching for comfort.

'My nose was bleeding when I woke this morning,' Will began again, thoughtfully. 'I get those nose-bleeds bad when I'm having nightmares because of something that happened a long time ago. When I got up I couldn't look at myself in the mirror. Faith knows it was my fault, Mitchell, yet she told me where she's living. She wants to see me again, even after what I did to her, what I let happen . . .'

The Radford & Doyle Institute was a large building out in the countryside. As well as a home for the blind it was also a sanctuary. There was a small school for the children, and some of the teachers had grown up there during previous generations, content to stay within the fold and not explore the outside world. There was a skeleton staff of sighted people who ran the kitchens and helped to manage the paperwork, plus a few teachers and lecturers who rented apartments within the complex.

After the death of the man who was killing blind women, Faith Gallagher asked Detective Will Bradley if he would take her back home to the Institute.

He held her, told her that men like that were few and that the world was not composed of evil, but had a heart of goodness.

A long time ago, Will thought now, as he sat on the beach and told Mitchell Ford what had happened, he had actually believed that. He had liked Faith, knew that her spirit was strong and he hadn't wanted to see her shut herself off in seclusion. He had wanted to take her dancing in the moonlight and speak the secrets of his heart . . . But he hadn't known how to. As a well-meaning but officious young detective, he had angered her so easily, simply by trying to help. She said it stifled her independence.

So he had agreed reluctantly to take her home.

* * *

The drive back to the Institute during a dark and rainy evening was a quiet affair, both searching for words that would express their feelings. Neither knowing what to say.

At the gates they saw Frank Sawyer, the nightwatchman. Over the several times Will had visited Faith, he and Frank had become friends, often indulging in a game of chess before he departed.

'You on for a game later?' Will asked.

'Got my board right here,' Frank said. 'I have my rounds to do so I'll meet you in the music hall.'

Will nodded. 'Be sure to bring your wallet.'

Frank laughed, throwing his head back. He was a big man, his voice deep. His laugh was like the thunder that crashed through the night, heralding the coming storm.

'You lovebirds get inside before the storm breaks,' Frank smiled, and saw both of his friends blush.

'Bye Frank,' Faith waved, and they left him behind, nobody noticing the headlights coming out of the darkness behind them like a pair of malevolent eyes, glowing white fire as they approached the grounds of the Institute.

So that they could spend the extra time together, they walked up the spiral metal staircase instead of taking the elevator. The elevators at the Radford regularly malfunctioned and chased each other passengerless. The couple dared to hold hands, a light contact.

'Do you have a girlfriend, Will?'

He studied her for a moment. Her young face was framed by cascading hair. Her skin was naturally smooth, unmarred by make-up, and she had a nose that ended in a slight ski jump. You're my girl, he thought. 'No.'

'Ever had one?'

'Nobody I was really serious about,' he told her – and that's what made this so much more difficult. He'd never been in love before, didn't have a blueprint to follow, no map of the human heart. He did things he thought were helpful and she ripped his head off. Learning the lines that he shouldn't cross was going to take time, and until he had them all marked he felt any relationship they began would fail.

'I don't believe you,' she smiled, and stopped.

They faced each other. In the giant skylight twenty floors above lightning flashed, decorating the night sky since the clouds were hiding the stars. They could hear the rain as it pattered onto the glass. The wind howled about them in the silence of the chamber.

They leaned closer. Lips touched. She felt a soft hand on her back and she wrapped her arms about him, not intending to let him escape now that they had finally found each other.

The kiss was long and slow and soft. Months of restraint leashing their passion.

It was a seal of their feelings, a promise that no matter how long they were apart, however long it took before they were ready, they would always be waiting, always dreaming for the day when they would finally be together.

They began to walk up the stairs again, their hold firm now.

'I don't believe you,' she giggled. 'You kiss like you've had a lot of practice.'

'Yeah, well,' he smiled, then realised that with Faith a lot of his boyish charm was wasted, 'I've kissed a few girls in my time. But I've never been in love.'

'Never?'

'Until now,' he told her.

The door opened into a corridor that was lined with doors on both sides. Down the hall an elevator door chimed open. Nobody got out.

'Who is it?' Faith asked, standing motionless. She felt his hand grip hers tightly.

'I'm sure this place is haunted,' he suggested. 'If the lifts are not broken, they go up and down all by themselves.'

'It's just the ghosts. Are you worried about him?' she asked. 'He's dead, Will. You told me.'

They were standing motionless. The elevator had closed and was continuing on its aimless travels, up and down all night long.

'Just a cop's instinct,' he told her. 'After more than a few years on the Force you get wary of the slightest things.' Will worried for a second: they never did recover a body, just assumed that the guy they had wasted was the one killing blind women. 'Come on, let's get you to your room.'

At the door to her room they kissed again. This time, he tugged her blouse free and felt her breasts heaving in his palm. She gripped his butt and pulled him close, could feel him press against her.

Then they separated.

'Come in,' she whispered, kissing him delicately on the mouth.

'Don't go in there,' he pleaded. 'Don't return here.'

'Your world frightens me, Will,' she told him. 'What you do scares me. I don't like it, can't be a part of it. Here I feel safe. This is my home.'

'But you're so isolated here – I need you with me. I'll always watch over you. Please – come with me.'

'I'm sorry, Will. I . . .' Faith began. *I love you.* 'I need to be here for a while.'

'We can find a place together, start a new life.'

'Soon,' she promised tenderly, and kissed him a final time, before he left her alone.

Waiting for the elevator back to the ground floor, Will stood in the empty corridor and wondered why he hadn't accepted Faith's invitation and gone into her room. He decided he was afraid – that he wouldn't know how to treat her right, to touch her. He told himself it would be the same as with a woman who could see, but he wasn't sure if that was true.

Will also wanted their first time together to be special, not sneaking around in the dead of night like a teenager sleeping over at his girl's house.

The pressures of any normal relationship were tenfold simply because she was blind – and because he often didn't know how to handle that situation.

For a moment he contemplated going back to Faith's room, wanting the decision to be made for him. Then he decided that she would already be sleeping. He would call her in the morning.

'Chicken,' he whispered to himself.

Thanks to faulty wiring and the storm outside, the elevators were trundling up and down the labyrinthine Institute without any passengers. One stopped in front of Will. It opened and he was stepping on board when a door slammed at the end of the corridor. Alarmed, he caught the closing doors with his hand before the elevator could move, and ran quickly towards the sound. He was thinking of two things.

One, they were yet to recover the body of the killer and identify it. Two, he had left his gun in his apartment.

The door led onto the giant staircase that was central to the building and which he'd recently climbed with Faith. Hearing pounding footsteps, he looked down just in time to see a hooded figure open a door two floors beneath him.

'Hey, you!' he called.

The man stopped and looked up. In the second before he hurried off the staircase, Will saw that he had a narrow face with thin eyes.

'Sonofabitch,' Will exclaimed, and began to descend the stairs. If only he had a torch, for the stairway was dim, the lighting erratic. An occasional crackle of lightning illuminated the way through the giant skylight. He tripped once, but caught himself before he could tumble down, and continued on.

He opened the door. The man was sprinting down the corridor. 'Hey!' Will shouted, running after him.

The man was wearing jogging pants and a sweat top with a hood. His clothes were wet and Will guessed he had been caught outside in the rain. His head bobbed as he ran and he slipped on the floor.

The hooded man was just on his feet when Will tackled him roughly back to the floor. The man tried to struggle away. 'I'm just the electrician,' he whined in a high-pitched voice as Will pulled him down. 'Don't hurt me!'

Faith undressed slowly in her room, thinking of Will Bradley. He was a man she cared for deeply and she wished fervently that he had come in tonight. For so long she had known solitude, but only now, missing him, did she know the true meaning of the word *alone*.

She lay naked on the bed and slowly began to tease herself, imagining Will touching her. One day he would, she thought. They would be together. But for now, she had only her fantasies, and her own hand.

She moaned quietly to herself as he entered her and pumped harder and harder as her fingers penetrated deeper. She rubbed herself on her fingers, gyrating her hips, her other hand massaging her breast, the nipple erect. Her back arched, the pleasure enticing.

Softly, she whispered his name over and over and began to sweat, stimulating herself as the fantasy continued . . .

And in a corner of the room, invisible and silent, the lightning revealing the white of his eyes, Dominick Rain watched. This was her most private moment, body and soul naked, and he was a witness to both.

This was the woman who was searching for him, he thought. Faith Gallagher. The one who was helping the police. He smiled, watching as she continued to arouse herself. She panted, pushing harder into her hand, moaning ecstatically as she continued the mantra of his name.

Killing her was a luxury he was going to enjoy. It was not a part of the mission his disturbed psychology had conjured up for himself. It was a time-out from his search for his mother, an opportunity to have some fun and make the rest of his life a lot easier.

Will took the electrician down to the main entrance hall.

'Go on,' Will instructed, pushing him out.

'It's raining, man. I'm going to get all wet again.'

'What were you doing working so late?'

The wind roared around them, blowing cold rain into their faces. The night was savage, biting at them with cold, razor teeth.

'Jesus, man. You're crazy. I'm going to catch my death out here!'

Bradley was certain this man was not the serial killer . . . *he's dead, you were there when he was shot and fell into the river* . . . but he could be some kind of deviant, a pervert who had somehow gotten into the Institute with the intention of harming one of the blind residents there.

'That your car?' Will asked as they struggled by a beat-up Chevy.

'You think I'd drive that piece of junk? You're outta your fucking mind! I live in a residence at the back of the main building. I was working late because I've got a bad case of insomnia. Now let me back inside. Leave me be.'

'Get in the car,' Bradley said when they reached his own vehicle. 'Two minutes and this will be all cleared up.'

Inside the man shivered. Bradley rifled through the glove compartment, spilling papers onto the passenger seat. He removed his handcuffs, instructed the man to hold out his hand.

'You're joking, right?' the man asked hopefully, and then added flatly: 'No. You wouldn't joke about this.'

The hoop clicked shut and Bradley rolled down two windows, one front and one back. He pulled the man's arms through on either side and then locked the second hoop around his other wrist.

The engine turned over once and then started. The drive down to Frank's booth at the main gate was a short one. During it, Will thought again of Faith. She would definitely be asleep by now.

'This is police brutality, man,' the electrician complained, wind and rain slashing into his face through the open windows.

'Shut up,' Bradley told him angrily, wishing he was upstairs with Faith.

They were only moving slowly in the bad conditions, but Will still had to brake suddenly when a figure staggered out in front of the vehicle.

Dominick Rain watched Faith walk naked from the bedroom into the bathroom. She stepped into the shower and pulled the curtain along the rail. For a few minutes he observed her shadow silhouette move as she washed herself.

Then, vigilantly and silent, he moved around slightly so that he could see her. She had smooth skin and a nice, trim figure. Her butt looked firm, and he imagined holding it tight in his hands.

He felt his arousal. This had nothing to do with the past, and what had been done to him as a child. Nothing to do with his good sister, Lorna Cole. It was something that had to be done – the death of a blind witness. Dominick decided he would enjoy the chore.

Lorna would never know he had slept around, and if she reluctantly accepted what he did to the blind women, then surely infidelity wouldn't bother her.

Faith turned in the water so that she was facing the stranger in the room. Rain didn't even flinch, merely admired her body, the pleasure and joys he would soon bestow upon it before taking her and dumping her in a shallow grave.

She was the only hope the police had of apprehending him, of ever realising that they had been tricked – *that he was not dead*. She was their only means of seeing. He smiled at the irony. Once she was gone, they too would be blind.

He removed the towel from the rail and tossed it into the bedroom. Then he waited for her to finish and the confusion and horror to begin.

This was the game. The towel must always be there, and now it wasn't. Somebody must have moved it. Who? Why? *Is somebody there?*

Sight is such a powerful possession, Rain thought. A weapon against those without it.

Will rushed out of the car and saw Frank fall to the ground. Blood seeped out of his body from several wounds.

Will couldn't find a pulse. 'Frank . . .' he gasped, his voice stolen by the wind.

Will ran to the booth. 'Jesus!' he groaned. There was blood everywhere. He tried the phone, but the line was dead. He sprinted to the car and quickly reversed it, the tyres squealing.

'Now where are we going?'

Will ignored his passenger and grabbed the car radio as he sped back to the Institute. 'This is Detective Bradley. I need an ambulance and back-up at the Radford & Doyle Institute. We didn't get him. *He isn't dead!*'

'What's going on, man?' They slid to a halt outside the building and Will feverishly pulled open the glove compartment before remembering that his gun was at his apartment.

'Shit!' he swore, slamming his fist on the dash.

He flung open his door and ran inside.

The police had been so easily fooled, Dominick thought, watching Faith, patiently waiting for her to finish. He knew every contour of her body now, and longed to touch it, to take her and finish her.

The man the police had killed was a homeless bum Dominick had picked off the street. Didn't ask his name, didn't care. They had shot the man in a classic case of mistaken identity. Dominick had then caught the body downriver. He quickly fished it out and put it in a grave he had dug earlier. Duped, they would never find it. Never even think of looking.

Until the blind continued to die.

The water stopped and Faith reached for the towel.

Dominick Rain smiled a secret smile.

Will waited at the elevators, paced impatiently, imagined them stopping uninvited and unwanted at floors on the way down, and then ran for the old stairwell.

Lightning flashed above in the giant window and the clouds rumbled. He took the first stairs two at a time, but it was a long way up and he was soon tiring. He pushed himself harder, tripped, knocked his head on the metal grating.

He almost lost consciousness, felt the staircase spinning about him . . . And then he was on his feet, running up and up, not pausing to catch his breath.

Faith's hand moved along the rail, searching for her towel. Habit – that was how every blind person lived. Things were always in their place, so that they were always to hand. The towel should have been there. With the water stopped, she was sure she could hear somebody breathing.

'Will, is that you?'

There were hollow drips. Final drops of water splashing down from the nozzle head. The thunder. *The wind* . . . Not someone breathing. She was alone.

The towel must have slipped from the railing, that was all, she assured herself. But her heart picked up a beat as she stepped from the shower, wanting to cover and warm herself. She bent. The towel wasn't at her feet.

'Will?' Her voice quivered. Suddenly she was afraid. 'Are you there?'

She walked quickly from the bathroom, almost running, but tripped over a chair that had been moved into the doorway. She fell into the bedroom and heard somebody snigger.

'Let's play,' Dominick Rain declared, advancing towards her.

She recognised the voice from her visions, remembered what had happened to Tabitha Warner and the others, the mess he had made.

Will raced down the corridor where he had chased the electrician, the lights still flashing. In an adjacent hall he spotted the man's toolbox. He frantically tipped it over, searching for anything he could use as a weapon.

He grabbed a large, pointed screwdriver and ran back to the Gothic staircase, tiring.

'Will is here,' Faith tried to say calmly, but her voice cracked twice and a sob escaped her.

'We're alone,' the voice assured her, suddenly close and she tried to crawl away.

Disorientated by panic, Faith found herself in a corner of the room, didn't know where the door was. Tabitha, she thought. This is exactly what he did to poor Tabitha Warner and the others . . .

The man laughed, and touched her for a few seconds with his hand, instilling more fear when he stopped, with the unknown prospects of what he might do next.

'Put on a coat,' he instructed. 'You might live a little longer.'

Faith trembled, tried to cover herself with her arms and hands, crossed her legs.

He suddenly cut her brutally. There was no way to know it was coming, and Faith jerked at the unexpected pain. She reached out, found his arm and grabbed him; reached out with her mind, focused all her energy. *Deep*, Faith thought, grasping him. *Look deep . . .*

A boy and a girl, just babies, days old, snatched from their cribs. The babies begin to cry, and wake the others. A crescendo of painful infant tears. The nurse; why doesn't the nurse come? She is dead — two bullets are lodged in her brain . . . The girl is carried by a woman, the boy by a man. Sirens fill the night, the babies are crying. The sirens are getting closer . . .

* * *

The sirens are getting closer. Reality intruded upon the vision.
Faith screamed, the blade cutting her again.

'Come on. We're leaving,' Dominick told her.

'No,' Faith cried, shaking her head. 'I don't want to play.'

'You never should have rolled the dice, then. You should have
stayed away – or do you like to watch what I do?'

'You sicken me,' Faith spat, turning away from his voice,
struggling.

Strong, brutal hands pulled her up, and she felt like those babies
being lifted from their cribs. He dropped the knife and forced her
into a long coat, then dragged her to the door.

He opened it and propelled her into the corridor.

Faith began to scream; Rain gripped her throat, and choked
her cries to silence.

A door suddenly flew open at the end of the corridor.

Rain pushed Faith against the wall and she collapsed down it.
The coat was flopping open and she hugged it around her body,
not wanting him to see her for a second longer. But, somehow,
she knew he no longer had time for her.

'Will,' she said with certainty, as the killer pounded away.

Detective Bradley spotted Faith, trembling on the floor, and
sped over to her, despite his thumping heart begging for respite
after the panic climb up the stairs.

Panting, he knelt before her and softly touched her arm. Faith
flinched away. 'It's Will,' he whispered frantically.

Faith struggled to pull the coat protectively around her. She
sobbed, didn't recognise his voice, couldn't hear his words, only
knew that he was a man, and it was a man who had done this to
her. She had to get away from him!

'Faith?' Will pleaded with her. He looked down the corridor,
saw her assailant had vanished, and then back to the woman he
loved. All the rape counselling he had learned from experience
and textbooks was a splinter in his mind that he could not get
hold of, buried in grief and hatred for the sick fuck who had done
this. '*Talk to me,*' he pleaded once she had settled a few feet away.

He moved to comfort her, but at his first touch she began to

81

rock herself to and fro, weeping brokenly.

'Don't come near me,' she sobbed, her body shuddering. 'Don't . . .'

Will watched her for a fleeting second, heard doors slamming and familiar voices in the corridors. The police had arrived. More sirens in the night. Suddenly, he knew what had to be done.

'People are here, Faith,' he whispered, 'otherwise I wouldn't leave you alone.' Tears were slipping from his own eyes now. He stared down the hallway, to the door . . . Where the man had escaped. No, not a man, but a purely evil being with a beating heart of dark intent. He had to be stopped. He had obviously fooled them once and they might never be this close again. 'Help is here. Please forgive me.'

He yearned to kiss her again, a light touch on her forehead, or to even just hold her hand one final time before he left. But he couldn't move.

'*I love you,*' he groaned, his voice a crack, like the lightning ripping the sky in two.

Faith merely mewled, her lips quivering: 'Don't . . .' It was all she could say. Over and over. 'Don't . . .'

Will stood, began down the corridor, but stopped at the door. He looked back for half a second. They had so much, he thought. There were problems, but they were beginning to deal with it all. Now he could not even comfort her, hold her through this traumatic ordeal.

Damn him, he thought, moving through the door, leaving her.

Will squinted into the darkness, the silence that greeted him.

Turn the emotion off, he told himself, freezing his tears. Think! The police are here; he knows that. He also realises that we are aware that he is not dead. He's afraid, scared that we might hunt him down with relentless passion, cage him. He won't risk going down, can't elude us that way.

Will looked up as lightning flashed in the skylight and thunder rippled through the clouds like currents through a lake. He started up the stairs. The roof was his only option.

Will clutched the screwdriver tight in his hand, knuckles turning white as he continued his ascent, a dark intent of his own burning an inferno in his heart.

* * *

Will caught up with the killer on the rain-slicked roof of the Institute. He tackled the man to the ground and pinned him down. Thunder rolled over them and the cold wind snapped at their cheeks.

Will hit him twice, the first punch breaking his nose, the second knocking him unconscious.

Silhouetted against the full moon that had absconded from behind the clouds, Will held the screwdriver high, prepared to plunge it deep into the black heart of the killer.

At the sound of sudden footfalls splashing closer, Will turned.

'Freeze!' Detective Chris Slater screamed, his voice rising on the wind. 'Drop it, Will!'

'He has to die, Chris,' Will called back, 'for all he's done. He tried to kill Faith.'

'Give me the screwdriver,' Slater instructed calmly. 'This isn't how it should go down.'

'He hurt her, Chris,' Will pleaded, hoping his friend would understand. 'He has to pay. It will prevent him from harming others. We can end it here. Now and for ever.'

'It's already over, Will. We got the bad guy. Let's just put him behind bars and watch him die slowly.'

'No!' Will shook his head frantically, his eyes wild in the moonlight. 'I can't let that happen. *I won't*. He fooled us once. He can fool us again.' And he clenched the screwdriver in both fists above his head.

'Enough!' Slater commanded, pulling the hammer back on his handgun. 'I mean it, Will. I'll shoot.'

'I know,' Will acknowledged, looking directly at his friend . . . and then he drove the screwdriver down, plunging the shaft deep into Dominick Rain's chest. Blood spurted into his face from the wound and he pulled the weapon free, red liquid dripping from it in the rain.

Thunder crashed, but the other detective didn't shoot. He couldn't hurt his friend for doing something he wished he had the power and passion to do himself. Instead he sprinted forward, tackling Bradley before the screwdriver could come down again.

They nearly toppled off the roof.

Will tried to get up, but Slater was a big man, who easily held him down.

'He has to die!' Will struggled fervently. 'Let me go!'

Slater brutally slammed his shoulders onto the roof.

'And he will,' Slater assured him, 'but not at your hands. Now *go*. I can keep this between us – we'll call it self-defence, but only if you get out of here. Go check on Faith.'

Her name shocked Will out of his violent rage. Suddenly, all he wanted was to be at her side, to know that she was going to be all right.

'Faith,' he whispered.

Detective Chris Slater let him up, and he ran to her . . .

'So what happened then?' Mitchell Ford asked Will, when he had finished talking on the beach.

Activity was picking up. Ford looked around uncertainly as tears slipped from Bradley's eyes. He had told Will he was here if he needed to talk; crying was not a part of the deal. Displaying emotion wasn't a strong card in Ford's hand; his wife had told him that much before walking out of the door, and he didn't intend to start now. Men with men, he thought with a disgusted shudder, wondering if he should hug Will.

But before he could move, Will sniffed and wiped his eyes.

'She shut me out. Shut everybody out. I couldn't get through to her, didn't know how to deal with it. I couldn't handle her not letting me near her. It was all my fault, and then when I got the opportunity I didn't even kill the bastard! So, I left. I only meant to go away for a short while, but the days turned to weeks, the weeks months . . . then years. Then I didn't know how to go back. Didn't know what I would do or say.'

'What happened to Dominick Rain?' Ford enquired.

'He went to jail. Still in there, as far as I know. I should have killed him, Mitchell,' Will asserted.

'You did try. But you didn't succeed,' Ford said, almost nonchalantly with a shrug of his shoulders. 'And now you're here, nearly two decades later, and you have to get on with your life.'

'What do you mean?'

'This,' Mitchell said, pulling Will to his feet. The older man emptied his sandals of sand as they spoke. 'Let's drink a cold beer or several, and then you can go find Faith Gallagher. Tell her how much you love her, and live happily ever after. It's obvious you should be doing that, even to an old, emotionless fool like me. It's some horrible *When Harry Met Sally* kind of thing you guys have got going. You've been apart for years and only now realise what you think of each other.'

Will laughed.

'Laugh it up, but I'm not joking. It's been nearly twenty years, Will,' Ford said again, 'yet as soon as she hears you are looking for her, she manages to get her address to you. I'd say that's a positive sign.'

'I do love her, Mitchell,' Will confessed to his friend. 'Always have.'

'Well, don't stand here telling *me* that – tell Faith! Now let's go get that cold one,' Ford said, and as they walked away, he put his arm around Will's shoulder, the best friend he had ever had, and punched him lightly on the cheek. 'Men with men,' he chuckled to himself. 'Who would've believed this shit actually works?'

The Gift

Last night, in my dreams, I had two visions, Faith Gallagher typed. *One of them featured the giant wheel I have written of before.*

In my first vision the wheel began to slow, and as it decelerated, I realised that this time it was actually the five blades of a heavy industrial fan, whirling around and creating a blurred circumference.

The fan in my dream was large and powerful, the edges looked sharp enough to cut and I felt sure it was moving towards me . . .

The second vision was even more compelling than the first because there is no way I can associate it with the revolving wheel. It is more troubling, too, because in it, I saw a man die.

I was shown high stone walls – castle walls, a voice informed me in my dream. Atop the battlements stood a man. He was of average height, with short, dark hair and the grin of a rogue. He looked confident, happy and—

Suddenly he falls, is plummeting down and down, screaming, wrists and fingers breaking, skin tearing as he grapples with the wall, searching for a grip that might save him. Down and down. Down . . .

Until, with a terrible impact, he lands on the ground.

Faith shuddered violently and took several deep breaths before resuming her typing. Tears shone on her face.

I must face these visions and search out the truth they harbour, solve the puzzles they present, she tapped out on the keyboard. *I have been hiding from this curse for far too long. I think about the objects in my basement. Sad memories given to me by bereaved families who have managed to track me down. I could have helped*

86

all of them instead of running. I must begin to see it as a gift, one
that can help people, perhaps even save lives . . .
    A light in the darkness to so many lost and unhappy people.

'Hey! Anybody at home?' It was Albert's voice, familiar and safe.
'Just your friendly neighbourhood biker come to call. Thought I'd
do some weeding before I went and acted mean at The Pit,' Albert
called out with typical good humour.

'They shouldn't be serving you at The Pit. You're too young for
that place. Come in,' Faith told him, releasing the lock, 'but please
be careful of the glass on the floor,' she warned.

'What glass?' Albert asked, closing the door.

'I dropped a glass and it shattered,' she explained, embarrassed.
'Over near my favourite chair.'

Albert smiled. Apart from the chair at the word processor, it
was the only seat in the room. Faith had once joked that she was
sure the store had especially moulded the cushion to fit her butt.

'Not a bad clean-up job,' he complimented her, bending to pick
up the few tiny shards she had missed. A sprinkling of glass dust
would have to be brushed. 'You haven't cut yourself?'

'I'm fine. Stop fussing,' Faith told him, hitting the Save key
hard, slightly irritated. 'You know how much I hate that.'

She switched off the computer which was especially designed
with a Braille keyboard and a printer capable of displaying Braille
and the alphabet.

'You're early, Albert,' she said, turning to him. 'What's
happening? You either surprise me, or arrive dead on the minute
you're supposed to. What are you up to?'

'Well, you know what they say. The early bird catches—'

'Who are *they*, Albert?'

'You know. *They*. They have advice or slogans for all occasions,
some of them a little worn by time now. They always have
something cool to say. The early bird catches the worm, or in my
case, gets a hot lunch date with Veronica Palmer from Denny's.'

'I'm losing you to the lure of an attractive woman,' Faith
laughed. 'Is she pretty?'

'She's got a great body, Faith. Breasts you'd die for,' Albert
grinned, and then apologised. 'Sorry. You personally probably

wouldn't die for them, but I'd give anything to have them in my—'

Faith held up a hand. 'I get the idea. What will you wear?'

'Veronica is a classy chick. I don't know why she's going for an oily guy like me. You think I should put on a tie, or stick with the rebellious biker image?'

'Is it an image?' Faith asked, wondering what circumstances could bring about a situation where a blind woman could be giving date advice to a teenager, especially when she was old enough to be his mother.

'No,' he told her, thinking for a second. 'This is me.'

'Then stick to what you are. She's going out with you, not somebody you might pretend to be,' Faith stated philosophically. Of course, I'm an expert on romance and matters of the heart, she thought cynically, still pining for a man I haven't seen in nearly twenty years. 'You'll do good. Now, what other gossip do you have for me?'

'Hey, you're not going to believe this,' Albert teased.

'I've shuffled to the edge of my seat. What is it?'

'Somebody died. Can you dig that?'

Albert was mature about his work for Faith, perhaps too mature sometimes, always checking on her, and he took his biking sojourns very seriously. But he was still young enough – immature enough? Faith wondered – to be excited about a death in town. He was eager for gory details, and less concerned about the effects it would have on the family or friends of the deceased.

'What happened?' she asked.

'I was talking to Paul – he's Deputy Kennedy's brother – and he reckons it was some dopehead kid who fell down a hole, into the sewage system out at Circle of Life.'

Faith cocked her head to one side, recalling the strange waking dream she had experienced recently, of a long, dirty-white truck moving swiftly along the highway . . . She had 'seen' its burly driver with his spider-web tattoo, only now the camera of her mind slowed over the logo on the side and saw it fully, for the first time. It showed an arrow trapped in the loop of a circle for eternity, chasing its own tail, pale lines blurring it, creating the illusion of motion and speed. In the centre of it, a flower blossomed, petals opening, a beautiful butterfly landing on it.

Circle of Life.

That, and the man falling from the castle, were somehow connected, Faith thought. *Some dopehead kid who fell down a hole.* She would have to contact the Sheriff's department.

'Albert, will you please give me a ride into town?'

'On my death device? I thought you didn't—'

'I changed my mind,' she said sharply.

'Hey, whatever you say, boss,' Albert said, jingling his keys.

The Ride Out

'Shouldn't I wear a helmet?' Faith asked.

Albert, revving the engine of his Yamaha, glanced over his shoulder. 'Get a good grip,' he told her, guiding her hands around his waist.

For the first time in her life, Faith didn't protest against help. She was petrified, and seriously considering climbing off the bike to call a cab out from the town.

'Lock your fingers around me,' Albert instructed.

'I'm ready,' she said shakily, realising that Albert was the only person she would trust in this situation.

Albert looked out at the rocky desert landscape, aware that if they went off-road they could shave almost ten minutes off their travelling time. His contemplation lasted only half a second before he decided to give Faith the ride of her life. Her very own rollercoaster.

'Hold on tight.'

The engine pitch changed and they jerked forward. The ride was slow and smooth for a minute, and Faith was beginning to think that it wasn't so bad when they hit the first bump. She jerked forward and Albert felt her cling tighter.

'Here we go,' he called over the noise. 'Just like *Magic Mountain*!'

They roared and bounced over the dusty landscape. Occasionally the bike would jump into the air and Faith felt like a bird, soaring in a crystal sky. The wind caught her hair and she screamed – surprising herself because it was with joy, the terror lost to the thrill. She whooped as the bike lifted into the air again.

After a few minutes, Albert slowed down. 'You can see your place from here, Faith. It looks beautiful. So tranquil.'

'Describe it to me, please,' she said, and felt the bike stop.

90

'It looks gentle. The sun is still climbing, the land is waking. Your home looks almost like a shadow on the horizon from here, a halo of light caught over it by the white clouds. Picture-book clouds, Faith.'

'Please stop,' Faith whispered, tears in her eyes.

'I'm sorry. I didn't mean to—'

'It's not you, Albert. I guess after all these years of living here, I'm still not ready to picture it in my mind. It sounded gorgeous, and the description you have given me will always be here,' she said, holding her heart, 'when I think of home. Thank you.'

They drove the rest of the way in companionable silence.

When they reached Cradle, Albert dropped her at the Sheriff's department.

'I'll find a ride home,' she told him. 'You go and prepare for Veronica. Have a good time. I want all the details tomorrow.'

'You bet,' Albert grinned, before roaring off, leaving her with the alien sounds of a town she hadn't visited for too many years.

The Department

The Sheriff's department of Cradle was like nothing Faith had experienced before. She had been expecting the hustle and bustle of a city precinct, the last frontier of a rotting world, and realised now that the police here were probably more used to rescuing cats from trees and dealing with simple domestic quarrels than confronting the horrific crimes she had experienced. The whole feel, the atmosphere here was different. This seemed like life in the slow lane of law enforcement.

Somebody even took her arm and gently guided her to a seat, taking the time to exchange small talk.

'A deputy will be here in a minute,' the man told her.

Almost as soon as he left, a different man with a hard-edged voice sat opposite her.

'What can we do for you?'

He seemed blunt, to the point. Arrogant. She took an immediate dislike to him.

'I would like to speak with Sheriff Louise Nash, please,' Faith requested.

'Would you care for some coffee?'

Faith sighed and remembered to be patient. None of these people knew who she was. At least in Denver she had had a reputation; people paid her attention and listened to all she had to say. But it had not always been that way. She thought back to the first day she had ever walked into a police precinct, back in Denver. People had growled like animals, the air was turbulent with the beating heart of violent crime. It had taken several hours to speak with somebody in authority, and several more before anybody took her seriously – after the discovery of another body.

That was when she had met Detective Will Bradley, the first

police officer to believe in her special abilities, and the first to act upon what she told them. And then he had taken on more than his share of the blame for the Bad Thing that had happened. The guilt had been a heavy weight on his shoulders, until it finally crippled him.

She missed him dearly. He had been a good friend, close, more than that, and for a few seconds, her guard slipping, she wondered what had become of him. Over a decade ago, a female detective in his precinct had told Faith of his resignation, that a lot of cops were talking about Detective Bradley in connection with something known as 'burn-out'. Other, more cynical officers said that he was on the take, that IA were sniffing around so Bradley had decided to get out while the going was good, but she knew that wasn't true.

Faith stopped searching the past and raised her head. 'I do not want any coffee, thank you. I *do* want to speak with Sheriff Nash,' she repeated, deliberately dropping the 'please'. This guy was no saint with his manners, and was beginning to irritate her.

'She's busy right now,' the voice explained sharply. 'We all are. We've got two dead bodies here. This isn't a typical sunshine day. Now, what can I do for you?'

Deputy James Kennedy studied the blind woman, saw her confident exterior falter for a second. He was sure he recognised her, but couldn't place the face. He had never known anybody blind and wondered if he knew her from his childhood, maybe slept with her as a teenager – before she had lost her sight. Or was it that her demeanour reminded him of somebody else?

'Did you say two bodies?' she demanded.

Just like Lou, he thought. They both seemed to have balls hanging between their legs, didn't realise they were women and should stay in their place, not poking their noses in other people's business or getting above themselves in the foodchain.

'I really don't think that is a concern of yours,' Kenny told her.

Faith smiled patiently, realised she was going to get nowhere with this man, did her best not to call him an asshole.

'*Faith?*'

She turned at her name and heard the man mutter under his breath: 'Here comes Queen Bitch.'

'Faith Gallagher?'

Faith stood. This voice was feminine, yet strong. She immediately felt better as the woman gripped her hand and guided her away from the obnoxious man.

'I thought I recognised you. Don't mind him,' the woman said. A door shut and the few sounds of the department ceased. 'I'm Sheriff Louise Nash. Please, have a seat. Albert called and told me you would be visiting.'

Faith decided Albert had a big mouth, but was glad since his communication had led to her rescue from the jerk.

'You said you recognised me. Have we met?' Faith asked.

'I saw the TV movie they made about you.'

'Oh, you were the one,' Faith replied with good humour.

'At the end, after making the big deal about you leaving the city and going into hiding, they went and played the credits over an actual photograph. Clowns.'

Faith nodded. Lo Goldman hadn't been happy at the screw-up. Faith decided she liked Louise Nash. Will Bradley had instilled the same warm feeling in her in the short time they had known each other. Comfortable. At ease. Secure.

'Down to business, then. How can we help you here?' Louise asked, pouring two cups of coffee. 'Or, how can you help us?'

'I have information about the dead teenager who was found at the Circle of Life pipe. But the deputy outside reported that there are now two dead,' Faith said sadly.

'That's right. First Ricky Turner – the teenager – and early this morning Walter Bascom pulled another body from Lover's Lake when he was dredging it for clues to the boy's murder. We haven't got an ID on this one yet.'

'I know that woman,' Kenny fretted, tapping a pencil against the telephone, trying to remember. 'I've seen her before somewhere.'

'I hope it was from before you started seeing me,' Deputy Claire Hobson said, sitting opposite him. She was a slim woman with breasts he had once likened to 'generous scoops of voluptuous flesh'. Her hair was tied back and freckles speckled her face around her nose, a few on her cheeks. She offered him a doughnut, but he shook his head. 'I can't resist these things,' she mumbled. 'This cream is to die for.'

'Can we please stay on the subject,' he told her.

'She's that lonely blind woman who lives in the desert,' Claire informed him.

'It's more than that.'

There was a silent pause and she started on a second doughnut.

'You keep going like that and you'll lose those cute buns of yours,' Kenny grinned.

Some girls didn't like that kind of talk, would slap you with a lawsuit as soon as eat another doughnut. Hobson didn't mind. She knew what the score was with Kenny, and wouldn't stay with him if she didn't like it. He treated her reasonably well, despite his misogyny, and had never laid a finger on her in anger, not like the drunken bastard she had dated before him.

She had cream on her top lip. Kenny resisted the urge to lean across the table and taste her flavoured kisses.

Claire finished the second doughnut. 'I know a great workout plan,' she teased, wiping the cream away and sucking her finger clean. 'We can practise it together later if you like.'

She left, and for a second he forgot the blind woman. He watched Hobson go, fantasising about what the workplan was.

And then, when Kenny's mind was off the case, he remembered where he had seen Faith Gallagher before.

Jack Ramsey

Lorna Cole was dressed in a smart navy suit, her short hair managed after an hour into a style she liked. It was in sharp contrast to the sleazy image she had deliberately paraded before Will Bradley. In this outfit her partners at the firm would recognise her. When she sat down in the Los Angeles restaurant she smoothed her skirt and casually let one heel swing from her foot when she crossed her legs.

'Hello, Jack,' she smiled. It was a nice surprise, if only because the FBI agent's call had dragged her out of a laborious meeting. Now they were preparing to eat before another gratuitous sex scene became a part of their life. They might not even get around to eating, she thought. Hoped.

Jack Ramsey was a handsome man, well groomed and muscular. But he had the personality of a pin, and his ability to charm a woman depended heavily on locker-room tales of sporting conquests. Unless he was talking shop – which was why she used him – Jack could be a real bore.

'You look great,' he salivated.

An attractive waitress approached but he waved her away, didn't even look, so captivated was he by the green jewels of Lorna's eyes.

She smiled, teeth white, tongue playing across them and her lips. He was so easy to manipulate. She knew she looked good, but this was nothing special. It was certainly a lot more classy than her sleaze-queen act, and she wondered how much Jack would like to see that. Probably a whole lot.

'Did you get her to sign the divorce papers yet?' Lorna asked, opening her jacket and the top button of her blouse. Playing games.

Lorna couldn't believe Dominick hadn't been in his hotel room last night. The last time she had seen him was through the glass partition of a penitentiary visiting room, palms flat, together, touching as if the heat of their love could melt the division. Now that he was free and they waited to rendezvous, time was passing extremely slowly, days stretching endlessly to nights, during which she either couldn't sleep or dreamed of him. She longed to look into his crystal eyes, a window to his tortured soul, which she hoped one day soon would be healed.

'No, I . . . I don't know how—' the FBI agent stammered.

'It's easy, Jack. You put a pen in her hand and tell her to sign her fucking name,' Lorna stated harshly.

'OK, OK,' Jack said, holding up his hand. 'I'll get it done.'

Lorna chuckled silently to herself. She could be a professional actress with a raw performance like that. She was certainly in the right town to give it a shot. She decided to cut her lover a little slack. Time to be nice.

'Thanks, Jack.' She held his hand. 'I'm glad you called.'

For a while they studied each other, ordered drinks and sipped at them. Sent the waitress away once more, both knowing the reason they met was not to eat, but to talk and fuck. Ravishing, undisciplined sex – captured energy, Lorna thought.

'Do you want to get out of here?' she asked him.

Inside the anonymous luxury hotel room there was no time for words. They quickly undressed each other, letting clothing fall on the carpet alongside forgotten inhibitions. They lay on the bed, Lorna pinning him down and taking control and then conceding to let him dominate for a while, rolling over onto her back. Fun and games.

She welcomed him, and as he pumped harder and harder, faster and faster, her fingers clutching and scratching, she thought of Dominick, and the reunion that would soon take place.

The First Seduction

Mike Castle sat in a diner on the east side of Cradle, the less affluent part of town. He looked out of the window as he sipped coffee in his private booth. A lot of the buildings in this neighbourhood were rundown, their windows boarded up, their doors hanging off broken hinges.

City-rot, Mike thought. Cradle was a growing town now; no longer the quaint little suburb all by itself. He finished his coffee and removed his notepad as a feral dog sniffed at a crumpled bag of litter.

Russell Crowe hadn't been home when Mike had first arrived in Cradle, beginning his search at Madeline's house. He needed that money. He remembered Madeline once talking about her friend, Nadine Sherman, and had quickly recalled her address. He asked a passing teenager for directions.

He found Nadine's home close to midday; he could hear a baby crying while he waited at the door. Nadine finally answered after putting the child down for a nap. While they had spoken in the living room she offered him cookies, coffee, and he remembered feeling slightly aroused . . .

Nadine enjoyed wearing feminine clothes, looking good. It was a complete contrast to how she had to dress for her smelly, sweaty job at Circle of Life. It was marvellous what a little silk and make-up could do. Some hairspray and perfume, and her spirits were lifted, the soft aromas carrying her into the clouds. She had been told to take a couple of days off after her morbid discovery out at Drain Pipe Three.

'Madeline's told me a lot about you,' Nadine said when Mike offered his hand and introduced himself.

Her shake was firm and Mike felt her nails on his hand; they were painted different shades of pink, gradually fading to a natural colour. He wondered what it would feel like to have those smooth nails on his back while they made love . . .

He smiled clumsily. 'Only the good things, I hope.'

'I didn't recognise you. From the way she spoke, I thought you would be wearing a halo, helping old ladies across the street, that kind of thing,' Nadine laughed. He did appear to be a good man, but she decided to knock him from the pedestal she had only just elevated him to. 'But I don't like that stubble. Don't you know that a modern woman prefers a smooth cheek, not that Don Johnson, *Miami Vice* bullshit?'

'Nice to meet you, too,' Castle grinned, assuming his best boyish look. He liked Nadine. She had a pleasant sense of humour and was instantly agreeable. 'I haven't slept all night, never even thought about shaving this morning.'

'I *bet* you didn't get any sleep last night! Madeline came over yesterday, wouldn't stop talking about you, all the things she was going to do with you.'

Mike Castle smiled disarmingly. Last night could have been his lucky night, if only she'd put in an appearance. Instead, he'd enjoyed the company of Roy Rogers and his pet retard, Trigger. At least he had gotten out of that one with all his bones intact.

Nadine continued. 'Even made me blush, the way she was talking, and that takes a lot.'

Nadine hitched her skirt up slightly, revealing more slender leg. Castle got a glimpse of thigh, and did his best not to stare. Was she coming on to him?

'Madeline never arrived last night,' he told her, hoping the conversation and mystery would distract him from her body. Although the prospect of communicating with Nadine at a carnal level was becoming vastly attractive to Mike, who just wanted to wipe the previous night from memory.

'What do you mean?'

'Why do you think I'm here?' Castle asked. 'I've come to find her.' *Find her money*, he thought.

Nadine smiled. *I know why you're here. Madeline told me what to do and say when you arrived looking for her.* 'But she went home to pack last night. Not that she wanted to take much.'

'Why didn't she want to bring anything with her?' Mike pressed, worried about the cash he needed for the cowboys.

'All Russell ever gave her was money and gifts. She was too good to him, too nice. Suckered in by it all.' Nadine paused thoughtfully.

'You don't like Crowe much,' Castle assumed.

'Let me tell you this. When Jimmy – my ex – walked out on me, I needed to find some work. Anything to put meals on the table and clothe my two children. Madeline put a word in for me with her husband, thinking she could get me some secretarial work at Circle of Life. Instead he offered me a job at the plant, manual labour.'

'At least you can feed your family now,' Castle observed without sympathy. He'd lost interest after hearing about the kids.

'He hits her,' Nadine went on passionately. 'Did she tell you that? She used to come crying to me and I always told her to leave him, but not Madeline. Everything would be fine for a few weeks, and then there would be new bruises, fresh tears. Do you think he might have seriously hurt her, Mike?'

Castle remained silent, wondering how much Madeline actually loved him, and how much she was merely seeking a way out of her marriage. If that was the case, why hadn't she shown up last night? Who was using whom in the relationship? They both had hidden agendas.

'Once she'd met you, she never came around to cry about Russell and what he did to her. She was always laughing and smiling. I've not seen her so happy in a long time. It's because of you, Mike. You rekindled her spirit. You are a good man,' she smiled, and her approval kept Castle warm inside as he left her house and climbed back into his car.

After visiting Nadine, Mike Castle remembered something Madeline had once told him.

Circle of Life hasn't saved the town. It's killing Cradle. In years to come, all that will be left is an island for Russell and his rich friends, surrounded by the waste the town has become.

With nothing else to do, Mike decided to visit the Town Hall, figuring he might get an easy story about company corruption in the town.

Now, sat in the diner in the late afternoon sunlight, he began to read through the notes he had obtained at the Hall of Records. He wasn't shocked by the industrial corruption he had found, having uncovered similar situations on many other jobs.

Those rich enough to invest in the Circle of Life chemical plant had done so wisely. Those educated enough had found employment with a reasonable pay cheque awaiting them at the end of the month, while others were hired to do manual work for a minimum weekly wage.

The rich got richer, and the poor and uneducated fell by the wayside.

The arrival of Circle of Life had given Cradle a new lease of life. It had survived. It would never die; except for the children of those who had built it.

Spike

It was that crazy bitch they made the TV movie about, Deputy James Kennedy thought. The one Lou had made him watch before she would even consider getting it on with him.

Lou didn't have that many vices or addictions, he reflected. But she did love those awful *TV Movies of the Week*. Invariably, by the conclusion, she would be blubbing at whatever true-life tragedy they had cheesily presented. The story of Faith Gallagher – crime-fighter and blind psychic extraordinaire, he sniffed sceptically – had been no exception.

It had been two hours after the film had finished before Lou relented and let him shake her bones a little – and even then he'd considered himself very lucky. Sometimes he would stay with her all night waiting for some action, only for her to fall asleep in his arms and then tell him the next morning that she'd had a great time, that it had been *so* romantic.

Well, if it didn't involve sex and a six-pack, then you could count James Kennedy out of the team line-up. He just wasn't interested. Lou had a good body, but with it came a bundle of morals and ethics, a complete package of feminine attitudes that meant shit to him.

He looked over at Claire Hobson, watched her filing papers. She noticed him staring and went cross-eyed. He laughed.

When Lou had kicked him out it had been a blessing in disguise, because then he'd realised the potential of Deputy Claire Hobson – a woman who also had a great body and didn't mind using it. Bonus. No strings attached, no deep involvement necessary, commitment not desired. Two people having a good time, treating each other nice. Nothing wrong with that.

Claire didn't mind if some nights, instead of her company, he

102

went out with the guys with the sole intent of watching sports and getting drunk as a skunk before retiring at her place. She didn't even mind if he puked down the sink during those nights, or whizzed on the floor; when he was under the influence, the size of the toilet bowl seemed to shrink, or there were multiple versions of it drifting in his sight and he didn't know which to aim for.

That used to drive Lou insane – but not Claire. She was special, he realised, gulping. She was his kind of woman.

And Faith Gallagher? Would she mind if he drained the lizard on the linoleum? She was a nut, he decided, getting back on track. She was becoming friendly with the Queen Bitch. Had to be crazy.

'Next thing you know,' he announced loudly to the room, 'she'll be taking her guide dog up to DP3 and have him sniff clues out.'

'For God's sake, Kenny. That's not funny! You can't talk about her like that,' Claire told him.

'I'm sorry to disappoint you, Deputy Kennedy, but I don't own a guide dog,' Faith informed him, entering the room unexpectedly.

'How did you know my name?' he asked, getting the jitters for a second.

'I know all kinds of things,' she told him, and thought back to the first time she had sensed the presence of Dominick Rain, stalking blind women like herself. Stealing life.

She didn't know his name then, who he was or what he had already done, for the curse had still been maturing. Yet it had revealed what Rain was capable of during the death of Tabitha Warner, and had imprinted on Faith's unwilling inner eyes the most horrific nightmare visions of madness. Prior to that she had sensed the death of a delightful German Shepherd – a guide dog with a playful attitude despite his serious role in life, called Samson. Samson had died when a bullet shattered his skull. A corner of the kitchen had been splashed with blood, flecked with brain matter and chipped bone. That was why she didn't have a dog of her own.

'Somebody could have just told you my name,' Kenny insisted, unaware of her bleak thoughts and memories.

Faith clamped a hand on his shoulder, gripped him vice-tight.

'Hey, lady—' Kenny protested, and then fell silent as he felt a grey cloud covering his spirit, an invasion of his most private feelings.

Faith tried to spike the power into him in an attempt to find the truth of the arrogant man, that he actually had a good heart.

She found nothing. A vacuum greeted her, a black hole sucking in all the light of his soul. She felt it begin to pull at her own energy.

Faith let go of his shoulder, jerked back as though jolted by an electric shock.

'Are you OK?' Deputy Dwayne Hicks asked, concerned.

Faith didn't hear him, wasn't aware that anybody existed in the room except for herself and Deputy James Kennedy.

'You are a bad man,' she whispered, knowing that only he could hear her.

'James?' Claire said across the table. 'Are you all right? You look like you've seen a ghost.'

'I'm fine,' Kenny stammered, wondering what had just happened. It was as if something had reached in and touched his very soul, and found it wanting. He spun suddenly. 'Get away from me, lady! Don't ever come near me again,' he hissed.

'Kenny!' Claire exclaimed, aghast. 'Don't speak to Ms Gallagher that way.'

'Never mind,' Faith said with a wave of her hand. Her composure was regained and she felt guilty at what she had done. 'Please take me out of here, Deputy Hicks.'

Searching For Will Bradley

Inside her office, after asking Hicks to take Faith Gallagher for a cup of coffee, Louise obtained a number for the Denver City Police Department. She punched it in.

'Hi, there. I need to speak with Detective Will Bradley, please,' she informed the man who answered.

'Please hold.'

She believed every word Faith had told her, and wasn't checking up on her background. She just wanted the opinions of somebody who had worked with her in the past. She would appreciate any help from a colleague to guide her in handling the unusual situation, especially with the kind of tension and pressures that were developing in her own building.

With such an important case – two bodies found in such close proximity – she needed the woman's very real abilities.

'This is Detective Gavin Phillips,' a different man said when a connection was made. He sounded bored. 'What can I do for you?'

'I think there's been a mistake,' Louise informed him. 'I need to speak with Detective Will Bradley.'

'You're about fifteen years too late. I was just a rookie uniform when he was here. I remember his name because there were lots of rumours at the time, about him dating that blind chick they made the movie about. The psychic one. What was her name? Is there anything I can do for you?'

'How can I get in touch with Will Bradley?'

'I can't even tell you whether he liked his doughnuts chocolate or fudge. I don't know him.'

'My name's Sheriff Nash, out in the town of Cradle, California. Can you track him down for me? You must have some records.'

'I'll see what I can do.'

Before she even had a chance to thank him, he had put the phone down.

The Drive Out

Ten minutes later, Louise visited Nadine Sherman at home.

Faith Gallagher had described visions of a giant wheel, which she had then deciphered as belonging to a Circle of Life truck, signifying the location of the dead body in DP3. They both assumed the man falling from the castle wall was Ricky Turner. Faith had then explained that the wheel had turned into a giant industrial fan. Louise wondered if somebody out at Circle of Life could be responsible for the murders.

She rang the bell and waited. The small front yard was looking better, she noticed. When Jimmy first walked out, Nadine had let the house and her life go to hell, but she finally seemed to be gluing the pieces back together. Louise hoped they would hold.

She rang the bell again and knocked on the door. Nadine finally answered, flustered. She didn't open the door wide, or invite Louise in. 'Hi.'

Louise thought the lack of invitation was unusual, but she could see enough through the crack in the door to realise that Nadine was dressed for a hot date.

'Who's the lucky guy?' Louise asked. She wanted to see more, but didn't want Nadine to know she was spying. Her limited view offered no information. 'I'm heading out to Circle of Life,' she went on. 'I sure could use a familiar face with me.'

'Louise, I'd like to help, but—'

'I'd appreciate it, Nadine. A friendly face with the workers. Somebody to keep Crowe's soldiers at bay while I check something out at DP3.' Louise had decided that Faith's vision of the fan might be pointing them to some evidence they had missed.

'OK,' Nadine said, resigned. 'Just give me a second. I have to arrange for a babysitter.'

Louise sighed, taking a step back to look at the front windows. Normally her friend leapt at the chance to do something together, and she particularly liked helping out with policework. Then again, who would want to go into work on their day off?

The curtains were pulled shut, but they were thin and transparent. At the back of the room, Louise could make out two figures. It was frustrating that she could hear the drone of conversation, but couldn't unravel any actual words, couldn't even ascertain the gender of Nadine's companion.

After collecting Nadine, Louise drove by the diner in her Maverick to pick up Faith Gallagher and Deputy Dwayne Hicks.

'I'm feeling quite ill,' Faith told Louise, while Nadine watched from the jeep, wondering what the blind woman had to do with anything.

'You going to be OK?' Louise asked, her concern genuine, not merely a courtesy.

'I don't know. I guess. We were chatting – appears you have quite a battle on your hands to win the respect of the people in your own department.'

'That's right,' Louise told her, and threw a sideways glance at Hicks, who silently nodded. Louise smiled; she had always believed that Dwayne Hicks, erstwhile football buddy of Kenny and fellow beer-drinking fanatic, had fallen in line with his Neanderthal peers in absolute rejection of her promotion. But now it appeared he had climbed over the boundary that separated them to stand beside her. 'Go on, Faith.'

'We were chatting up a storm, but I suddenly came down with something, out of the blue. I don't know what it is, but my stomach is still doing somersaults.'

Louise looked outside. Nadine was using the mobile phone she kept in the jeep. When she noticed Louise, she pointed at her watch and stared hard. Louise wondered what was getting into her friend; she was usually so casual and easygoing. Even through the divorce, life had never been a burden to her. But, from the variety of expressions while she used the phone, it looked like she was trying to solve all her problems via a single conversation. At one point she even looked afraid of what she was being told.

Who are you talking to? Louise thought. Who was in your home?

'It's not a problem. I think you can sit this one out. Deputy Hicks – will you drive Ms Gallagher home? Nadine and I will take care of business out at Circle of Life.'

The drive out to Circle of Life – whose motto was *Making the World a Better Place to Live* – was a mercifully short one. Nadine still seemed distant, her worry and mood almost tangible, and Louise was anxious to see if Faith Gallagher was right in thinking something else might be found near the fan. Her own stomach was performing somersaults.

Perhaps the company was making the world a better place, she reflected in the silence, but only by degrading the integrity and the environment of the town in which it was situated. Her hometown.

She shook her head.

'What's wrong?' Nadine asked, staring out of the window at the rocky desert landscape, still annoyed with herself that she had let Louise drag her back into work on a day off, especially with the company she had back home. She was now wearing jeans and a patterned shirt with running shoes. She didn't want the jerks at the plant ogling her, drowning in their own drool. She didn't really care what Louise was pondering, but knew the head motion had been a pantomime act intended to elicit conversation.

'I'm just amazed at the crap they are pumping into Lover's Lake,' Louise said thoughtfully. 'I mean, that place used to be beautiful. I used to take my boyfriends out there.' She grinned ruefully. 'Never let them get all the way. God, that must have frustrated the hell out of some of the ball players, but we sure had some fun.'

'All of our generation used to date up there. It was a place to go where we could be alone, with other couples in cars ranged up and down the banks.' Nadine smiled slyly, sharing teenage memories, and thinking of other moments she had always kept private, emotions that were resurfacing thanks to current events.

'What are you thinking?' Louise asked.

'Nothing, really.'

Recently, Nadine had seduced Kenny after Louise had dumped

him. That hadn't been difficult. A few beers inside him, and Nadine was sure Kenny would sleep with anybody wearing a skirt. The sex had been quick and passionless, Nadine hoping to find a small piece of Louise still on him. Her aroma, her flavour. She had been disappointed, but sometime in the night, before he passed out, Kenny had mentioned that Lou had been a virgin before their first night. That thought – the sweet fantasy of being with Louise at that moment – had provided Nadine with exquisite pleasure when alone, satisfying herself.

Nadine had given in to temptation early in life. She might not have been good with numbers, couldn't spell if she was paid by the letter and had a grade average that followed a falling curve – but she did know how to party, and had graduated with honours in pleasure.

Nadine remembered many times when members of the football team or the athletics committee had returned from Lover's Lake, only to ask Nadine what her best friend's problem was. 'Does she actually like guys?' some of them had said meaningfully. Nadine would laugh, flutter her eyelashes a little and promise them a better time if they accompanied *her* to the lake one night. During those times she would hope to catch a taste of Louise's kisses in their mouths, jealous as she was, of every last one of them.

'Come on, we never used to keep secrets,' Louise reminded her friend in the Maverick.

I've always kept secrets, Nadine thought. From you, from everybody. From the world. 'I'm just remembering, that's all.'

Louise had been so square. Nadine realised she had been building up barriers between herself and her friend even then, fencing her off because even though she was so close, she would always be so very far away. Forever unattainable. She wished that she had acted on the impulse that normally fuelled her all those years ago at Lover's Lake when she . . .

Nadine closed her eyes momentarily. One day she might find the guts to tell Louise what she really thought, what she should have told her many moons ago, when all around them, wild teenagers were getting drunk, getting laid . . . And she was dreaming of the girl in the car next door.

They were supposed to be soul-mates, born seconds apart and

110

all that other poetic bullshit their parents had frequently spouted. But there was a bridge of sexuality between them; Louise would never cross it, so until Nadine did so, the bridge would always be there, bitterness building upon growing resentment, making it even harder to reach out. Some romantic comedies played the premise that a guy and a girl can never be just good friends because the sex part will always eventually get in the way, and Nadine felt the same for Louise, the secret she had kept bottled up for years once more bubbling on the surface of her mind and threatening to explode out in the Maverick.

Nadine did as she always did, channelled her jealousy into other feelings. Louise the success, playing Town Marshal, running around Dodge City like she was Wyatt Earp. She stared at her friend with contempt. You think you're so much better, she thought.

'So who was the guy at your place?' Louise asked breezily, unaware of her friend's mixed-up mind and pent-up feelings. 'We never used to keep secrets,' she repeated.

'I was home alone,' Nadine lied. She had met somebody, and it was that relationship which was dredging up all her old feelings for Louise.

'Oh yeah?' Louise laughed, and Nadine was glad because it meant her friend would lay off with the prying questions. Louise's laughter was the sound of chiming church bells over a snowy landscape, and her smile was so sweet. Nadine wondered – as she often had when she was a teenager – what it would be like to take Louise up to Lover's Lake and dominate her, show her a new sexual awakening, before they would lie together and fall asleep in dreams scented with perfume.

'Louise, have you ever wondered what it would be like to sleep with a woman?' Nadine asked, biting her tongue at a question she never meant to ask.

Louise faced Nadine for a second, before concentrating once more on the straight road. She saw that Nadine wasn't joking.

'Not really,' she answered, the question unexpected. 'No. Never. Why? You thinking of asking me out on a date or something?'

Nadine gave her friend a casual laugh. 'No,' she said.

'What's wrong?' Louise asked, sensing despondence in Nadine.

'I don't know. I guess the memories are coming back a little too fast now. It's something I used to think about a lot, usually after Jimmy had bruised me, before we would go to bed. I used to dream about curling up next to somebody who was . . . God, this sounds so corny, I can't believe I'm telling you this.'

'Nadine, those fantasies must have gotten you through a lot of hard times. But just because you got unlucky and ended up married to Jimmy the Scuzzball, don't wipe out the whole male gender. Besides, a lot of women can be real bitches.'

'Yeah, you're right,' Nadine responded thoughtfully.

'It's human nature. Some people are born good – others bad. It's the way they are. Others get mixed up along the way. But women and men can be equally evil. Gender has nothing to do with it.'

The Fan

Sheriff Nash was wearing a green outfit – pants with tight elastic at the bottom of the legs and a thick top – she had found in Nadine's locker.

'It can get quite crappy down there,' Nadine warned her, and she wasn't wrong, Louise reflected, shifting slowly down the declining crawlspace.

She could have walked up the entrance of Drain Pipe Three and checked out the fan from the tunnel, but she wanted to get an up-close look and the wire cage would have prevented that.

The stench was overbearing, almost enough by itself to make her want to turn around. The clean handkerchief she had tied around her mouth and nose – like a Western outlaw hiding her features – was completely ineffective. She could taste the thick odour. On her hands and knees, she was grateful for the thick gloves Nadine had insisted on loaning her. She didn't understand how her friend could tolerate working in such conditions. Kids to feed, or not.

The flashlight flickered and she paused, tapping it onto the close wall. She silently applauded herself for not panicking, for keeping her breathing steady. She was plunged into darkness again and then the torchbeam thankfully flickered back on.

She wished she'd thought to put new batteries in before she came down here.

Louise calmly moved forward. She tried to look back up the narrow pipe, but could barely see around her own body. There was no room. What if she got trapped down here? Her heart began to pound. She felt sweat break on her forehead. She shouldn't be here. This was a stupid idea. She could—

Shoes are ruined, that's for sure, she grinned, her mind

unplugging the claustrophobia. No matter how hard she scrubbed them clean, that terrible smell would always permeate through the leather.

Still she smiled, aware that she had managed to ward her phobia off for a short while. She could sense it stalking her down this dark pipe, with walls that could collapse any second; she could feel its cold touch on the nape of her neck, tiny hairs tingling.

She scurried on, sensing the phobia's close pursuit. If the fear gets hold of you, it will choke your energy, suffocate it, leave you frozen here, trembling in an endless night. *Move fast*. Don't let it catch you.

Then she stopped, and looked up. The fan was close. She could make out dirty details in the metal blades. She swallowed; her breathing was steady again. She had faced her fear and survived. She had made it.

Louise remembered Nadine's locker-room caution as she strained between the motionless blades of the fan.

It used to run on a timer, but that's busted. Crowe's too cheap to fix it, so the fan just switches on and off whenever it likes. It'll take your fingers off, Louise. Be careful.

So long as it doesn't come on now, Louise thought, her shoulder pushing onto the blades as she awkwardly reached through. Would there be any warning? A chance to move before the blades started rotating? Or would they simply spin around and take her arm off?

She was grasping for two pills which she had spotted in the beam of her flashlight. The white capsules must have bounced through the wire grating of the cage, landing in the thick sludge near the fan. A rat was ignoring her, trying to nibble through the wire with needle fangs. She gulped deeply, hoping there was no more vermin in here with her.

Her fingers tickled the medication, and she watched with horror as one of the capsules sank into the mud. She'd never find that one now. She stretched for the other.

She wondered if this was the reason Faith had fallen ill – a sign that some kind of medication would be found down here; a clue to the killer's identity.

Suddenly, a heavy ratcheting sound echoed down the pipe. She jumped, and the fan moved slightly, then gathered momentum until her arm stopped the blade. But she could already feel more pressure as it built up speed.

'Shit,' she whispered.

She clenched her teeth, sensed the fan cutting into the sleeve of the thick top; pulled free.

Within seconds the fan was whizzing around, mashing the sludge, breaking it down, and her arm with it had she been foolish enough to leave it there.

Louise leaned against the wall of the pipe for a moment, claustrophobia forgotten as the fan blew a cooling breeze into her face. That had been too close. She looked into her palm; shone the torch on it. She pushed some of the muck away, and there, almost magically, like a precious pearl, lay the lozenge-shaped white pill.

Louise laughed with relief, dropped it into a small evidence bag and sealed it.

'What are you for?' she whispered. 'Who do you heal?'

Once they had established what the medication was for they could check hospital and pharmacy records to see which townsfolk had been prescribed the medicine. This would supply them with a list of local suspects, although that did not rule out the possibility of a drifter.

It would help once they had an identification of the body from Lover's Lake. She was sure Bobby Fullton would have that information by now.

Louise began to crawl out of DP3, her ascent slow and careful, to keep her cut arm off the ground. She did not want to infect it.

Back in the changing room, freshly showered, naked and cheerful, Louise removed her uniform from Nadine's locker. She noticed her friend staring at her in the mirror that had been taped onto the back of the metal, vented door. Nadine was stood at the far end of the steel aisle. She looked like she needed somebody to talk to.

'What's wrong, honey?' Louise asked, easing into her blouse, her muscles crying out after the cramped conditions.

'Nothing,' Nadine said shortly, and left the room before Louise turned.

'Hey,' Louise called, stepping into her skirt. 'Wait for me!' Nadine was definitely worried about something, she thought. They needed to have a heart to heart, just like the old days. Soul-mates all the way to the very end.

Louise spotted some perfume in the locker and reached for the bottle. God, now she understood Nadine's pleasure in dressing up and feeling feminine after a long day at work.

Louise shut the locker and went in search of her friend.

The Opportunity

'I have to go away,' Jack Ramsey told Lorna Cole, lying on his back, exhausted. 'I'm sorry. It's an assignment. There's nothing I can do.'

Lorna lay beside him. Her eyes were emeralds in the shadows; her body lithe, sheening with sweat. The sex had been satisfying, but that was not why she kept a lover in the FBI. Often Jack helped with her private investigations – he had helped her locate Will Bradley, for instance – via his connections with the Bureau, and more often his loose tongue supplied her with interesting, if superfluous, information.

'For how long?' she asked, staring at the ceiling, wishing she was with Dominick.

'I don't know. A few days, maybe more. Maybe less,' he said hopefully, and then hesitated. 'Lorna, I'd like to call you while I'm gone.'

She smiled. His little boy act could be really sweet sometimes. 'You don't need permission, honey. Just pick up the phone and punch the right buttons.'

'No. I mean, I'll miss you,' Jack stumbled, rolling to face her. 'I love you, Lorna. When I return I'll get my wife to sign the divorce papers. I promise.'

'Where are you going?' Lorna asked, not even smiling.

'Some nothing town called Cradle.'

Lorna rolled onto him, her interest piqued. She sensed his arousal, felt it rubbing on her. '*Cradle?*' she repeated. Shit! How could she go there with Dominick if Agent Ramsey was going to be hanging around all the time? He would surely see her. Could Dominick even risk seeking his vengeance now?

'Yeah. There's been a double murder. The Sheriff's department has requested our help,' he explained, his loose tongue flapping away. 'We've still got some time, though.'

Jack reached under the covers, but she grabbed his hand and abruptly pulled it to her mouth. She sucked his finger for a second and then let go and climbed from the bed.

She dressed quickly, long legs slipping into her skirt, anxious to be out of the room. It was imperative that she talk with Dominick *now*. He had better be at the hotel this time. They needed to move fast. If Ramsey made it to Cradle he could ruin everything, all their plans.

'I'm late – I have to go. Call me,' she told him, and was out of the door, a new idea already forming in her mind.

Immediately after leaving Jack, Lorna placed two calls from the nearest payphone.

The first was to a man named Donald Blythe, whom she had successfully defended a couple of years ago. He was a superb forger, who could produce good work quickly. He owed her and she was calling in the favour now.

Lorna had a lot of contacts in the underworld, as well as those in positions of authority. But she had only ever loved one man. She had dedicated every day of her life to him, and the time of their reunion was now imminent.

If Dominick killed Jack Ramsey, he would be able to assume the FBI agent's identity. Nobody in Cradle would have reason to doubt him.

Her second call was to her brother's hotel room. He was in, and she greeted him with the good news. She had not only found Faith Gallagher, but was about to provide Dominick with the perfect cover for when he arrived in Cradle.

Identification

'Hi, Louise. Had a good day?' Deputy Dwayne Hicks said cheerfully when Louise returned to the department building that evening.

'Dwayne, I want you to listen to me very carefully. No, I have *not* had a good day. I've spent over an hour crawling through some serious toxic garbage, and I've ruined my favourite shoes, which happened to cost seventy dollars.'

Louise moved to the water cooler and filled a plastic cup.

'That's an expensive pair of shoes. Bobby called while you were gone.'

Louise looked around. Once the shifts had changed over, the night duty was usually a lot quieter than the day. But this silence was ridiculous. They were the only two people in the building.

'Hey, where is everybody?' she asked, slightly mystified, but already suspecting what was happening.

'Robinson and Curly called in sick – some kind of flu virus. Francis, too; wife said the same shit. The rest of the night crew is on patrol – all two of them. And they were complaining about not feeling too good.'

'Kenny,' Louise said slowly.

'I stayed over to answer the phones, but now you're here I'll be heading home,' Hicks told her, grabbing his battered leather jacket and throwing it on. He got as far as the door.

'Wait a second,' Louise said, motioning for him to come back.

'Yeah?'

'You said Bobby called,' she prompted.

'The ghoul said that the body Walt found in the lake had three bullets in him.'

'Did he give you a name yet? Time of death?'

'Sure did. But if you had a bad day so far, it's not about to get any better.'

'Give it up, Hicks.'

He paused. 'Russell Crowe.'

Louise sat on the edge of the nearest desk, held her face in both her hands and sighed deeply. God, what was happening in her town? She had hesitated before calling in the FBI, wondering whether she was being rash, but now she was glad. Russell Crowe was a rich man, powerful with his money. His death was going to bring additional pressure to her department.

'Are you going to tell his wife tonight?' Hicks asked.

Louise sagged, remembering her visit to Ricky Turner's family that morning, the trauma her news had induced. 'Let her be tonight. I'll inform her tomorrow,' she decided. 'What was the time of death?'

Hicks grabbed a stale doughnut from the desk of Claire Hobson. He pulled a face at the taste, but he was starving. 'Not got it yet,' he mumbled, then held up his hand. 'But Ricky Turner checked out less than a day before he was found. That's why he was never reported missing. I almost forgot – Fullton said that Crowe didn't die from the bullet wounds. His lungs were flooded; he drowned.'

'So he was still alive when he was put in the lake,' Louise said, disgusted. There was a good chance Crowe had been unconscious and the killer believed him to be dead already. But what if he was groaning, trying to struggle . . . That was ruthless. The act of a depraved mind.

Hicks made to leave once more.

'Hold on,' Louise called.

Hicks looked back, didn't return this time, remained in the doorway. 'I do have a life outside of here,' he said truculently.

'I can't leave until somebody comes in for the graveyard shift. I need a favour,' she told him, her expression pleading, looking for sympathy. 'Just one. Will you do it?'

Hicks hesitated. She wanted an answer upfront which could only mean he probably wouldn't like what she was about to ask him to do. But she was going to be stuck here for a while, and all he had to go home to was a six-pack in the fridge and a TV dinner. It was no big deal. He nodded.

Louise rummaged in the pocket of her jeans and tossed an evidence bag to him. He caught it casually in one hand and studied its solitary contents. A lozenge-shaped capsule covered with speckles of dirt.

'On your way past Bobby Fullton's office, drop that in and tell him I could use some results tonight. If not, then first thing in the morning.'

'But his lab is across town,' Hicks protested. 'It isn't on my way.'

Louise smiled. 'It is now.'

Reunion

'I want a room for the night,' Jack Ramsey told the clerk. 'Also, I need directions to a town called Cradle. I got lost in this pissy weather. I mean, do we still live in the Sunshine State, or what?'

'Actually, you crossed into Nevada about fifty miles back. The rest is not a problem, my friend,' the scrawny man behind the counter responded, starting with the directions. Over his shoulder, through a crack in the door, Jack could see that he had a porn channel tuned to a tiny portable in the small, cramped office. The reception was bad and the image rolled every few seconds.

He thought sourly of his wife, then smiled at thoughts of Lorna Cole.

Jack paid the man and picked up his keys.

Crazy weather, he thought, going out into the rain. Storm like this in the middle of the desert – it was ridiculous. The hard rain slashed into his face, cold and stinging in the early hours as he jogged briskly down the line of cabins, never noticing the car that had arrived while he was obtaining a room. It was barely visible, its headlights dead, parked on the far side of the lot. The two occupants strained to see him in the dark. They were holding hands, their grip firm like teenagers first realising how much they liked each other.

They were both afraid to let go, after so long apart.

'Come on,' Dominick Rain whispered eagerly, moving to open his door, but she held him back. She could see the need for vengeance in his eyes; the death of Jack Ramsey the first active step to completing his goal.

Lorna had become intimate with Ramsey while acknowledging that she was only using him, but the thought that the agent was about to die was troubling her.

She recognised that none of this was a good thing. One day, they would both end up bullet-ridden or in prison. The spirit of goodness that she had harboured within, her sacred humanity, could never triumph over this evil. Yet she needed Dominick, and knew that his cold heart would never thaw and warm until Faith Gallagher was dead in the ground.

'Once this is over, Dominick,' she began, softly stroking his chest, 'I want us to lead a normal life. I want us to find our own paradise. There have been times when I wondered if what you did was all wrong, if they ever should have let you out. If you had any true motivation for the murders, other than . . .'

'Don't you remember what they did to us?' he asked anxiously.

'I remember,' she whispered. How could she ever forget? But through it all, she had managed to find a sliver of humanity, and as much as she loved Dominick, she didn't want him tearing it away. 'Let's just sit here a while.' She kissed him lightly. 'I've missed you so much. Let's just hold each other, my darling, and when the killing is over, we can hold each other for ever.'

She dreamed of that, clinging together in the car, a dry world in the rain. After all the horror, all the blood that was yet to spill, they were finally going to live happily ever after. Just like in the fairy tales she used to read to him, when he would sit on the edge of his truckle bed, a blindfold on, still bleeding from the latest beating, until the candle finally flickered out and the darkness swallowed them both.

'Happily ever after,' he whispered, calm before the raging storm.

The Last Seduction

'What the hell is this for?' Mike Castle asked, rummaging through Nadine's bag. He pulled out the large handgun he had found by accident. 'Make my day,' he intoned, aiming the weapon at her.

'It's for shooting people. And it's loaded,' she cautioned him, 'so point that thing someplace else.'

Mike held the gun at his side and posed before his hotel-room mirror, pretending to draw like a gunslinger.

'Really, though. What gives with the hardware?' he insisted, repeating his actions. 'This isn't a big city. I bet the biggest crime around these parts is when the old ladies cooking for the Sheriff's department manage to burn the cookies.'

Nadine sighed. How little you know, she thought. 'When Jimmy left me I thought it might be best if I had some kind of . . . home defence.'

'Most people settle for a dog.'

He continued to admire the weapon. The only time he had ever seen guns before, up close, was when the henchmen of various loansharks were shoving them up his nose. It felt nice being on the other end of the barrel for a change.

'I didn't come here to play cowboys and Native Americans,' she smiled, catching his eye by unbuttoning her blouse.

'What are you – Dirty Harriet?' he laughed.

'You'll see how dirty,' she told him, removing her blouse and then her bra.

Mike instantly put the gun down, remembering why he had been in her bag in the first place. *Protection*, he thought. She said if they were going to do anything, they had to have . . . He watched Nadine as she stepped out of her skirt, couldn't help grinning like an idiot because she wasn't wearing any panties.

This was like some kind of teenage fantasy.

'Hurry, Mike,' she whispered, taking slow, delicate steps towards him.

She was close now and Castle was beginning to sweat. Coming to Cradle had been no mistake, he decided, his hand finally wrapping around the small packet he was searching for. He had eluded Roy Rogers and that dumb shit partner of his, the one that thought he was a horse.

And now this.

He admitted that he hadn't found Madeline. Nor did he have any money.

Nadine held him firmly at arm's length, pushed him roughly up against the wall.

'I've thought about you all day,' she murmured, peeling his shirt off. 'Is this wrong?'

But who cared about Madeline at a time like this? he thought.

'No.' He swallowed deeply as she began to unbuckle his trousers, letting them fall to the floor. He shuddered as she pulled down his shorts and fell to her knees before him.

It wasn't as if he was engaged to Madeline or anything serious like that. He was only in the relationship for the money. He was a guy, and Nadine was a beautiful woman who had come knocking on his hotel-room door in the middle of the night with the sole intention of . . .

He looked down, caught her eye, her painted face like a china-doll. Gorgeous.

'You've been on my mind all day, Mike. You make me feel giddy as a schoolgirl on her first date. I bathed before I came here. I imagined your hands washing me. Touching me, all over . . . *Touch me, Mike.*'

Nadine reached up and took the condoms from his hand.

'Let me put one of these on for you,' she whispered, kissing him.

Fifteen minutes later, Nadine retrieved the used condom as she had been instructed and left Castle singing happily in the shower. He had been easy to stimulate and she was glad it had ended quickly. She had hated every second he was within her, every second she had spent in that horrible room.

She ran to the nearest telephone booth, at the end of the parking lot, and made the call.

'It's done,' Nadine panted, catching her breath from the sprint, afraid that Castle would follow her out when he realised she was gone.

'Good. There's one last thing for you to do tonight, Nadine.'

Nadine looked around angrily. 'It's supposed to be over already!'

'Tomorrow it *will* end, when you send him to see me. Then we just have to wait until the will is—'

'What do you need me to do?' Nadine sighed deeply.

She listened to her instructions, knowing that she would obey them without question. It sounded like a simple task. Breaking in would be the difficult part, but at least she wouldn't have to hurt anybody this time, she thought, closing her eyes. It was just going to take half the night, that was all.

'I'm tired of running your errands,' she protested. 'We were supposed to be doing this together.'

'And we are. While you've been out having fun I've put your children to sleep. Do you think I like spending time with brats? Stanley's OK, but the one that craps everywhere . . . Jeeze! I hate cleaning that shit up. It's like the toxic waste you have to work in, Nadine.'

'Tough,' she said cynically, checking to make sure Mike hadn't come out looking for her. She should have gotten away from here before calling home.

'Don't complain, honey,' the voice wheedled. 'You won't have to stay there much longer. Soon we'll have—'

'Don't talk about it,' Nadine snapped. She hated what she had done, all that she had become. She wished she had the guts to tell Louise. Tell her everything . . . but that wouldn't help her children.

The money would. And soon they would have the money. Then she could get her family out of Cradle and try to put this nightmare behind her.

'OK. Let me talk about something else. Without me, Nadine, you'd be grovelling in that shithole for the rest of your life. Your children wouldn't be able to go to college. They wouldn't even have decent lives. Without me—'

'Enough, please,' Nadine protested on a sob. The world was so very wrong. It had twisted on its axis and everything was spinning in a vortex, events wildly out of control. She wished that Louise could comfort her, that none of this had ever happened.

'You don't sound very happy, Nadine. When you come home I'll give you something poor Mike Castle never could. Satisfaction.'

Nadine put the telephone down with shaking hands. My God, what had she done? She thought about going back to the room, telling Castle to get out of town, leave before it was too late.

But that would ruin everything.

The guilt was bad enough, but if she saved Castle then it would all have been for nothing. She would have to flee Cradle with her children, in a battered station wagon. They would have no money after she had come so close to setting them all up for life. Money . . . that was what this was all about.

There was one bad deed left. And then all her bad deeds were done. There was only a life of goodness ahead. She wouldn't have to harm anybody ever again. Not ever. She could sit by a sky-blue pool and live off the interest. Her children would achieve their dreams.

She walked back to her car, her eyes wet and red, but smiling through the recent tears.

Think of the money, she urged herself. Think of the future – the security and opportunities you can provide for your children.

My children . . .

Thinking of them, and what she could give them, made all the bad deeds in the world worthwhile. Any risk worth taking.

PART TWO

Blind Fear

The Lost Children – Two

Lorna convinced Dominick to let her enter the motel room first.

She walked across the parking lot, not bothered by the rain, concentrating on what she was about to do, wondering what she might say. Jack Ramsey had done nothing wrong, except fall for her seduction. And now he was going to die for it. Lorna wanted it to be easy for him. No pain. She had to kill him now to prevent him suffering a violent death at her brother's hands.

She also knew that with his death, there would be no turning back. This was the point of no return. She had campaigned for years for the release of Dominick Rain; it had been her own private crusade, for her own very private reasons. If she walked away now, she would be betraying her whole life, all she had ever done since the days when they were children and she used to nurse him in the dark. All that would have been for nothing. Her life would be one big, bad lie.

She contemplated this, considered walking out onto the highway and not looking back, while she waited for Jack to answer the door.

Dominick would not stop until he had avenged his incarceration. Throughout his years' imprisonment, Dominick had branded the impression of a single woman onto his eyelids so that even when he closed his eyes and slept he would always see her. Faith Gallagher. He would never sleep peacefully until Faith Gallagher was dead and was haunting him no longer.

But would it end there?

He had given Lorna a solemn promise that the killing would stop, that he would get better no matter what the cost. All he asked was that she help him finish this matter, even though she might get blood on her hands.

'We'll live a normal life. Have children, treat them right. Buy a little house with a garden and a picket fence. Anything you want, baby,' he had told her in the car.

But did she believe that?

She could remember many reasons not to . . .

Lorna Cole smiled as she climbed from the car, ran across the street and nearly tripped on the kerb. She looked back as her friends pipped the horn, cheering and waving out of the windows. She grinned happily and removed her heels before she even considered tackling the steps into the apartment building.

Her life was finally looking good, she thought, entering the building. Sure, they lived in this pit, and Dominick had had some problems assimilating into regular society – but after all that had happened, after all they had endured during a traumatic childhood she had expected this, was surprised that she was holding up so well herself. She had just won her first solo case; was proud and very drunk. At the moment she could beat the world.

Once inside the apartment, all she wanted was to run a hot bath and fall asleep in the soothing water. She carelessly kicked off her shoes, knowing that Dominick would tidy up behind her in the morning, and put a light on.

Her patterned blouse was sweaty and reeked of cigarette smoke from the bar where she had consumed several celebratory Martinis. She began to unbutton it as she walked to the bathroom, and then stopped short when she saw what was in the tub. Something that stared up at her with bloodshot eyes. Dead eyes that did not see the light.

The woman was naked and large, but not obese. Her hands were tied together behind her back, her ankles tied in front with thin wire that cut into her skin. Her body was smeared with blood. She had not been dead long; the aroma rising from her was not unpleasant – in fact, it was the scent of perfume.

Lorna vomited straight into the toilet bowl, falling to her knees. 'Dominick!' she screamed. 'Dominick!'

'I didn't hear you come in,' he called from a different room. 'Don't go into the—' He appeared in the doorway. 'Oh. You've seen her.'

132

'You can't . . .' Lorna stammered.

'I found her,' Dominick smiled, himself naked, bloody. 'I didn't want her to hurt any children like she hurt us. So I stopped it.' He looked proudly at what he had done and moved past her, to switch on the shower. Water began to rinse blood from the body.

'I killed her in the tub because it would be easier to clean up afterwards. I remembered what you told me last time, about the mess I made in our old apartment,' he explained.

'Dominick,' she cried, dragging him from the room because the sight repulsed her. That poor woman, what had he done to her? 'Mother's dead, remember? You already killed her and set us free.'

Dominick looked blankly at Lorna.

'She was going to do it again,' he protested. 'I had to—'

'You have to remember, Dominick. They locked us in that hateful cellar from when we were babies. They let us up into the main house sometimes, but only to serve them. And we were never, ever allowed outside. Think back.'

Dominick began to scream like a child. Wordless noise. He waved his hands in the air. All he wanted to do was shut out the words, stop the truth. He didn't want to know what happened, didn't care. He was here now, and he had done what needed to be done. That woman would have hurt the children.

'She was going to—' he protested.

'*No!* Listen to me!' Lorna grabbed his arms and looked directly into his eyes. 'Listen and remember. You saved us from that place. One time, we were down there for days and nights on end. Nobody brought us food.'

Dominick nodded slowly. 'We would have died.'

'That's right. But you knew that. You broke the door down and . . .'

Dominick closed his eyes, picturing the knife in his hand even as she described what he had done to his own mother and father, who had punished them too much for far too long for so very little.

'. . . and then we came out of the darkness, into the world for the first real time. It was like being born again. We ran into all that open space. The silence after all the screams and tears. The silence was beautiful. Serene. You must remember the clouds?'

133

Dominick smiled happily. He had run into the hills and tried to touch the sky, the beautiful objects floating within it. For all his life the ceiling of the cellar had been the top of his world. They were suddenly thrust into all this majesty. They ran and danced with joy and made love under those clouds, celebrating their freedom.

'Clouds,' he whispered, smiling at the happy memories. He looked so sweet, like an innocent child.

'Remember two months ago?' she asked him.

Dominick's face began to quiver, tears rolling silently from eyes that were suddenly shut tight.

'You killed that blind woman. You brought her back here for me. You were so pleased at what you had done – but what did I tell you, Dominick? *What did I say?*'

Her words were frantic. She had to get through to him. He had to stop killing.

'No,' his voice cracked.

'Think, Dominick,' she cried pathetically. 'You have to tell me why this is so wrong.'

'I can't remember!'

'Please . . .'

'I don't know!'

'Dominick . . .' she sobbed, and then gathered herself, held him gently. She made eye contact again, drilled into him so that he had nowhere to turn, couldn't look away. 'Not all blind people are like Mother. Most are good, honest, hard-working. Mother was bad – and Father, too – *before* she lost her sight. I used to have dreams when we were down in the cellar, of the world we found outside the house, of being held up to the clear, blue sky in strong hands when I was little . . . There are good people in the world, Dominick, and bad people. Which would you rather be?'

'I want to be good,' he whispered.

'Good and bad, Dominick. Blindness has nothing to do with it. *You have to stop this killing.* Do you hear me? Do you understand?'

'I messed up!' he suddenly sobbed, his red chest heaving. 'I didn't mean to kill the lady. I thought she was hurting children . . .'

'Do you understand?' she repeated calmly, emphasising each word.

He nodded.

'Come here, then,' she whispered softly, hugging him. Holding him tight. She didn't care about the woman's blood smearing on her. She swallowed deeply. What she was about to say repulsed her. 'You have to stop killing, Dominick. Fight whatever urges you have. But if you *need* to kill . . .' She closed her eyes. 'If you *can't* stop, I still love you, Dominick. After all we've been through, I'll never leave you. If you *must* kill,' she repeated, weeping, 'don't bring them back here. And don't ever tell me about it. You have to promise me that.'

'I do. I'm sorry . . . I didn't mean to hurt her.'

Lorna took his hand and led him to the bedroom. 'Let's make things better, and then you have to clean up.'

He shivered at the phrase. There were some things Mother and Father had made him do that he would never tell her about.

She undressed and they made love, the blood of the dead woman on both their bodies. It was slow and tender.

Then Dominick cleaned up his mess and disposed of the body. Come morning, when she woke, the apartment was pristine.

Lorna prayed that it had all been a bad dream; one that would not visit her again in the dark hours of night, or in the light of day . . .

Now, waiting outside the cabin, Lorna considered grabbing Jack and running with him to his car. Or taking him to her brother, telling him what Dominick intended to do.

All her life had been strange, bizarre, perverse – through no fault of her own. She had always fought against the deprivation and depravity, reading books and comics, anything she could get her hands on in the horrible house; anything she could smuggle into the cellar. Dominick had accepted their fates, wallowed in the darkness.

Once in the real world, she readily began to enjoy the aspects of normal life she had always been curious about. Watching movies. Eating at restaurants. Going on dates. But through it all she had never forgotten Dominick. Would always love him. Never leave him.

What they had shared and had together was a forever thing. *Special*. They had a love and bond unlike anything on the planet. They were destined to always be together. From the time of their grisly childhood, locked down in that terrible room – even in years to come, holding hands, old and awaiting their own deaths, they would never be able to live without each other. Or escape that hateful place, for it would always be a part of them.

Lorna took a deep breath, knocked on the motel door and swallowed deeply, preparing to kill Jack Ramsey.

The Date

Veronica Palmer leaned towards Albert Dreyfuss; their first kiss was memorable. Slow. Deep. Soft. Wet. Three days long. Finally they came up for air and his hands began to fumble at her clothes.

Lunch had gone very well earlier that day.

The food was great, the kind a teenager would call classy before his tastebuds mature and he discovers real restaurants, with actual menus and waiters. The kind kids love. Greasy. Messy. Fattening junk. They both ate two burgers and double helpings of fries, with large milkshakes.

Albert spent some time wondering how she could manage to eat like a pig at the trough and still maintain such a great body.

Conversationally, they hit it off. There were no awkward silences, no stilted gaps between topics. They had similar tastes in music and movies, although she was more critical. They had similar dreams and ambitions, although she was eager to implement hers while he was happy living in a cave for a while longer. He spoke of his parents, the reason he stayed out there, and she didn't consider him nutso – as some of her jerk friends called him, a freak for living differently – but the most compassionate guy she had ever met.

They left holding hands and went for a walk in the park. They had ice cream and after sitting together for a couple of hours near the lake, she told him she had to go into work.

'Can I see you when you've finished?' Albert asked.

'Pick me up at midnight.'

He did, although she finished nearly half an hour into the witching hour. She climbed onto the back of his bike and they rode out of town and into the desert. She screamed with joy, felt the wind in her long hair. She whooped, her heart pounding with fearful adrenaline. She held tight, and hoped the rocky rollercoaster would never end.

Lying under the stars in the early hours, after the kissing and fumbling was over, she was glad that it had.

They were about half a mile down from his cave, on a small plateau. Beneath heaven itself, Veronica thought.

She giggled.

'What's wrong?' Albert asked, wrapping his arm around her naked body.

She smiled. There was a chill in the air and his arm was warm. So was his body. They pressed against each other.

'I wonder if the gods blushed when they saw what we just did,' she pondered. 'I wonder if they were watching, or if they turned away.'

Albert stared up into the deep sky. The stars; a million and one pin-holes in the thick curtain of night. He knew what she meant. Often, he wondered if his parents were up there, their souls a pair of the twinkling buttons, watching over him, no matter what he did, or where he went.

He hoped they hadn't been looking just now.

He kissed her and they lay still.

Veronica yawned. 'This place is so perfect, I could easily fall asleep here,' she whispered, lightly lifting off him. 'But I'd better not. I have to get home.'

'Stay the night.'

'Don't beg,' she told him, quickly pulling her jeans on.

'Please,' he laughed, kissing her sandy feet.

'Never beg. All good things come to an end.' She pulled her T-shirt on. 'Get dressed. You can give me a ride home.'

'You forgot these,' he said, holding up her panties and bra in the moonlight.

'Don't worry. I'll get them off you tomorrow,' she said, slipping into her shoes. 'Hurry. I don't want my parents interrogating me.'

'Tomorrow?' He began to dress.

She helped him with the zipper on his jeans, reaching inside. 'Yeah. You do want to see me again, don't you?' she grinned confidently. 'I think you do.'

'What time should I pick you up?' he asked.

'Don't bother. It's my day off. Be here all evening tomorrow and I'll jog up sometime. Surprise you.'

'Jog up? Do you know how many miles we are out of town?'

'Don't worry about it. Just be sure you're here all night because I don't know what time I'll make it. How do you think I keep my figure and still eat like Roseanne Barr?' she asked rhetorically. 'Will the stars be out tomorrow?'

'The stars are always out,' he murmured. 'This is heaven.'

Our Stars

When Louise finally returned home late that night, Wade had already fallen asleep, his blond hair falling unkempt across his closed eyes.

Maximillian Othello – Max, her clumsy, cuddly Doberman – was restless, so she played with him for a while in the backroom, fighting for his squeaky toys. Exhausted after the late games, he panted, tongue lolling out of his mouth, and padded to his cushioned box. Max fell asleep instantly, leaving Louise covered in thick slobber.

She showered, thought of Bobby Fullton, disappointed that he had not called about the pills from Drain Pipe Three yet. Then she made a sandwich and went into the bedroom, contemplating Wade as she slowly ate it.

She pushed her thoughts of the day away. All she wanted to do was admire what she had, be with Wade. She needed him to be inside her, wanted to feel alive and loved after the dark day.

'I love you, Wade,' she told him softly, kissing his forehead.

He stirred and moaned quietly, but his eyes didn't open. She kissed him on the mouth.

'Umm,' he whispered groggily. 'Why so late?'

She placed a finger on his lips and began to undress. He reached up to help with her clothes, but she pushed him back down and climbed on top of him.

The stars were out, a thousand different worlds illuminating the night, and the bedroom through the giant bay window. This view is ours, Louise reflected. This was a moment they would remember all their lives, holding each other, watching the glorious sky.

For these blissful minutes she could be on a different planet, the horrors that had come to her town forgotten.

A twinkling star fell from the sky while they watched, trailing a thin stream of light.

'Starlight, starbright, burning through the sky tonight. I wish I may, I wish I might, have this wish, I wish tonight,' Louise recited softly.

'Where did you learn that?'

'It's a poem we used to say when we were children. We used to lie on our backs at night, looking directly up, waiting for stars to fall.'

'Did you make a wish?' Wade asked, kissing her ear. She nodded. 'What was it for?'

She smiled. 'If you tell a wish, it will never come true.'

'I'll make it come true,' Wade promised her. 'I love you, Louise. I already have my wish.'

'I love you, too, Wade.'

The Little Girl

I can see the little girl again.

I saw her for the first time late this evening, after Sheriff Nash had visited to tell me about the pills she had found.

All I saw then was her freckled face, framed by long soft hair. She was standing by Drain Pipe Three staring at me intently. She looked sad.

I don't understand how she can fit into all this.

Upon the visit of Sheriff Nash, my stomach was no longer upset. We both agree that the illness was psychosomatic, brought on somehow by the gift. I have never known it to work on such a subliminal level.

And now the girl . . . Who is she? What can she have to do with the deaths of Russell Crowe and Ricky Turner, the teenager?

Faith woke suddenly, her heart pounding, certain she had heard a noise. She relaxed slowly at the silence which greeted her, the sledgehammer in her chest relenting.

Dominick Rain is in prison, she assured herself. Whenever she was alarmed in the night, that was always the first thing she thought. He wasn't here. Couldn't be. She must convince her mind that—

A brutal hand clamped over her mouth and she was dragged off the bed, sheets coming with her. Her head hit the floor and for a second she was dazed. She felt blood at her hairline. Before she even realised what was happening, a rag was stuffed into her mouth, stifling the scream that was rising in her throat. The coarse material was taped across her mouth.

'Shut the fuck up, lady!'

Male. Deep and rough. Strong, too, to have pulled her from the bed like that.

'Listen carefully and you won't get hurt,' the man hissed.

He forced Faith onto her stomach and then sat on her back. She tried to estimate his weight as he twisted her arms back. He wasn't heavy, and she thought she might buck him off, but then he had tied her hands together, tight, the thin rope burning, and was rolling her over.

'You be a good little girl and stop snooping. Otherwise, you might have an accident!'

She tried to kick away, felt her foot connect with the man's jaw. He let out a surprised cry, high-pitched, and then quickly tied her legs.

'Bitch,' he whispered harshly, close, hitting her with an open hand. 'You remember what I said!'

And then he was gone.

She listened to him move out of the room, out of the house. She heard an engine. A car – nothing like a motorcycle.

Faith trembled on the floor.

She struggled to get free, but couldn't. The knots were too tight, cutting into her.

Lights on, she tried to whisper. But the gag choked her voice and the computer didn't recognise her. *Lights on*. If Albert woke in the night, was still up with his date from Denny's, he might see the light, get curious and come down from his cave in the rocky hills.

Lights on! she cried, the sound muffled.

But the computer didn't answer.

The engine sound had faded into the night now. He was definitely gone.

She relaxed on the floor. There was nothing else she could do. She fought the knots for a while but couldn't get loose.

She thought about the man who had attacked her, replaying the events over and over. Something puzzled her, something not quite right about what had happened.

He could have killed me, she thought. He's killed two people in this town already. Why not me? I was dead, if he wanted it so.

She would talk to Sheriff Nash in the morning, and she would suggest this: whoever had killed Russell Crowe and the teenager had a motive. The dead men had not been murdered by a thrill-seeking drifter. Their deaths served a purpose.

But that was not all that perplexed her.

She felt blood on her cheek. A slap wouldn't have ripped her skin like that, unless he was wearing a ring. Or maybe his nails had broken the skin.

She struggled again with the ropes, twisting her feet. Getting nowhere. When she had lashed out, her foot hitting him, catching his jaw, he had sounded like . . . She couldn't put her finger on it. He had let out a squeal, like . . .

The pitch of his voice had fluctuated a lot. He was under a lot of stress. Threatening a blind woman can't have been part of his original agenda. It had sounded like he was trying to disguise his voice.

The shivers stopped and she relaxed again, giving up her fight against the ropes. She was safe. In the morning Albert would find her.

She actually began to drowse, there on the floor, her hands cramping painfully. She dreamed of Will, wondering if he would ever come for her, wondering why the man had disguised his voice, what he might be hiding . . . and then dreamed of Will again.

Casting out into the night with the power, searching for him, beckoning him to her.

Will . . .

Deadly Affair

'Lorna!' Agent Jack Ramsey exclaimed when he opened the motel door. 'I was just thinking about you, honey. What are you doing out here?'

'Aren't you going to ask me in?' Lorna said, choosing a life with Dominick, accepting all the risks, the lunacy, so that they could be together again. He might stop, she thought. He really might. After Faith Gallagher the killing might end . . .

'Come in,' Jack offered eagerly, closing the door behind her. 'Now what's all this about?'

They kissed and she smiled guiltily. 'I followed you, Jack. I needed to see you. I needed to tell you something.'

'It couldn't wait until I got back?' Jack laughed. God, this was great. This was the kind of spark and spontaneity that he missed when he spent time with his wife. He felt his erection surge and kissed her again. 'I spoke to my wife before I left. She's promised to sign the divorce papers while I'm away. When I've finished in Cradle we can start thinking about setting up a home. Maybe getting married.'

'Jack,' she said solemnly, 'call your wife. Tell her you love her.'

Jack looked confused. 'What—?'

She pushed him onto the bed. 'Call her. Tell her that you are sorry for screwing up. That you love your children and will miss them.'

'What are you talking about?' he demanded angrily.

'Jack, do this last thing for me,' she insisted. She couldn't let the agent die without his wife knowing what he actually felt. He had fucked up big time, been led astray. Without her the couple would probably still be together. She wanted him to put that right, fix things before . . . 'I promise, Jack, we'll never be

145

apart again if you do this one thing for me.'

'But I thought—'

She kissed him hard and handed him the telephone. 'Make the call,' she urged.

He hesitantly punched in the number and watched her walk to the window, look out.

She was glad that Dominick was still sitting in the car, on the look-out for her signal. She didn't want Jack to suffer.

'I still don't understand,' he said, waiting for somebody to pick up. 'Is this some kind of game?'

'Hello?' a little girl said.

'Hi there, pumpkin,' Jack greeted his daughter.

'When are you coming home, Daddy?'

'Soon, sweetheart. What are you doing up so late?'

'Watching cartoons. Do you want Mommy?'

'Please, pumpkin. Be good and go get her.'

Jack watched Lorna turn slowly. She had a gun in her hand. A Walther PPK, equipped with a silencer. She aimed it at his chest. She had tears in her eyes.

'What—?' Jack began, looking for his own gun. It was in the holster hanging on the back of a chair, way across the room. Shit, he thought. He wouldn't even get off the bed.

'Hello?'

'It's me, Tina.'

'Just who I wanted waking up by. Why don't you get lost, Jack? I mean it. I've—'

'Honey,' Jack began, and froze. It wasn't going to be difficult to convince her. He *did* love her. You always realise how much you need or want a person when you are about to lose them, he thought.

'Go on,' Lorna whispered, attempting to redeem herself for what she was about to do. Make up for seducing him away from his wife and then killing him. She couldn't cry. Blinked back the tears.

'Is somebody there with you?' Tina asked.

'No. It's just . . . the television. I love you, baby.'

'I don't want to play games any more, Jack. I told you I would sign the papers.'

'Make her believe you,' Lorna hissed.

'Do you have a woman with you?'

'What? No. Tina, I love you. I seriously fucked up. I really did. But you have to believe me,' he implored.

'Jack, are you drunk or deaf? *I don't care.*'

'Listen to me. I messed things up for us in a major way. You'll . . . shit. You'll probably see it on the news.'

'What are you talking about?'

'Understand this, Tina. It's important you listen. I love you. I always did. I'm sorry I fucked up for us,' Jack said quickly, tears slowly falling from his eyes. 'Tell the children I love them. That if they ever want to talk to me, I'll be listening. I'll hear them. We had some good times, didn't we?'

She paused. 'Yes.'

'Tina—'

'Jack, if this is serious and not some dumb joke for your latest girl, then call me in the morning when you're sober.'

'Don't put the phone down,' he said frantically. 'Don't hang up!'

'Goodbye, Jack,' she said, and put down the receiver.

'I'm sorry, Jack,' Lorna told him, hesitated, and then pulled the trigger.

She walked to the window and opened the curtains. When she saw Dominick get out of the car – spotting her signal – and run towards the cabin she closed them again, and then let him in.

Without words Dominick moved the body into the bathroom and covered it with the bloody sheets.

He then went to her, and they made love for the first time in over fifteen years. It was hard and desperate, against the wall before they slipped to the floor. Frantically they exhausted each other.

They could never live apart, Lorna realised, lying on the mattress. Couldn't exist. It had been a mistake to even consider it after struggling through all those years without him. Despite having lovers, friends, she hadn't been complete until this night. He was a part of her, and all those years he had been imprisoned, a part of her mind had dwelled there, too.

The second time they made love, waiting for the forger to arrive with Dominick's new identification papers – the ones that would state his name as Jack Ramsey, an agent of the FBI – it was very slow and careful.

She remembered the first time they had been together, down in that pit – an excavated cellar in which their parents had confined them to eternal darkness – when they were teenagers and had found exciting, tender ways to comfort each other. Arousing feelings and emotions they had never felt before in their cold, dark world.

Together they could defeat anything. They could face the giant universe after their closeted world, and survive.

Now they would never be apart again.

'I love you,' she whispered when their fifteen-year hunger for each other was temporarily satiated.

'I love you too, Lorna,' he told her softly. 'Even when they held me captive, you waited for me. I don't know what I would ever do without you.'

'You'll never be without me. We're meant to be together.'

'I don't know how much longer I could have survived on my own. It was like being down inside that pit again, only without you to hold me and guide me. Without your human touch. I was afraid I would never see you again,' he sobbed.

'I'm here now,' she soothed, holding him. 'I'll always be here.'

Their love was undying and meant to last for ever, she decided.

They held each other for a long time, until they heard a car pull up outside.

Donald Blythe, the forger, had arrived.

Return To The Cave

Once Albert had dropped Veronica at her home, sharing one last kiss on her porch, he had roared out of town. All he could think about riding home was the wonderful night he'd had, and the fact that he would soon be seeing Veronica again.

Before reaching the point where he would get off the road and race over the landscape to his home, he passed a station wagon. He wouldn't normally have paid it any attention as it headed into Cradle, just somebody travelling late, looking for a place to get some sleep, but he thought he recognised its battered exterior from town.

The woman inside was crying, not concentrating on the road, swerving wildly and he slowed while she drove by. She saw him, realised he was looking in, and tried to shrink back into the shadows of the moving vehicle . . . which was then gone.

Sketches

After drinking the afternoon and half the night away with his buddy Mitchell Ford, Will Bradley returned to his Hollywood office.

'You still chasing ambulances?' Miss Garibaldi called from across the street.

But Will could not respond; he merely nodded. He staggered up the steps, and told himself it was because of the dark and not the drink.

After all that had happened, his desertion of her, how could she possibly still want to know him?

He unlocked the office door, made it to his desk and fell heavily into the chair. He sat there for a long while, thinking of Faith and all he had done, reliving all the guilt trips he had spun out for himself across the years. He had left her instead of trying to fix things, instead of being patient and waiting for her to work things out in her own time.

But after coming so close, after finally seeing the true way they felt for each other, he couldn't bear to be shut out any longer.

He dozed. Woke later with her name on his lips. He whispered it to the empty room.

He began to draw, his pencil scribbling quickly across the paper.

A couple of hours later, he noted that all the regulars were lined up across several pages.

Jean Luc Picard, bald of pate and half his face vanished behind Borg technology; Will Riker, a charmer with his sax in Ten Forward; Geordi Laforge, witnessing life through his visor; Data, a happy smile as he searched for the truth of humour; Worf, mean and menacing, and ugly as a Klingon; and then the women – Beverly Crusher, Deanna Troi, and even Security Officer Tasha Yar, each beautiful and gorgeous and scantily clad.

All three of them, he now noted, bearing an uncanny resemblance to Faith Gallagher.

It had been years, yet he could still see every detail about her, every nuance, and he began transferring it all from his mind to the page, his pencil moving in a feverish state.

He stopped after completing several images.

Faith stared up at him.

He suddenly missed her so much – a feeling beyond measure. He animated her face in his imagination, making her features move. Then he made her speak. In his drunken condition it was easy.

Come to me, she appeared to whisper. *I miss you, Will. Please come to me. I need you.*

He needed to see her, just to look at her and know that everything was all right. That she was well. Safe. He didn't even know if he could speak to her after all he had done. His cowardly neglect.

But he had to see her.

Come morning – he didn't want to risk driving in his current condition – at first light, he would head for the town of Cradle. It was a trip he had to make.

And then sleep came easily and he had good dreams of the life they might have had together. A life that still might be.

Day Three – 0901

Captain Chris Slater

The report left by Bobby Fullton on Sheriff Louise Nash's desk was short, and took her only a few minutes to scan through.

The pill she had found was called Jericho. It was used to ease arthritic joints and to prevent muscle aches. The report established that neither Russell Crowe nor Ricky Turner were taking the drug. Bobby had contacted their physician Dr Bale – saves me the call, Louise thought, glad that some people were still on her team. There were only two deputies in the building.

The results of Bobby's enquiries were disappointing.

Dr Bale had said that only three people in town were currently prescribed Jericho. One was a seventy-year-old man who couldn't walk without the aid of a frame. The second was a woman with a badly twisted ankle. Both of these were unlikely suspects, but the third was a potential candidate. He was a teenager – the same age as Ricky Turner – by the name of Zach Galligan.

However, he'd broken his leg and for two weeks it had been in a cast. The report continued that Galligan had displayed an allergic reaction to the pills. They had caused his stomach lining to bleed which had induced severe vomiting, and so for the past week he had been using a different form of . . .

And so it goes, Louise thought. Either the pills were irrelevant, or an outsider had killed these people. She sat down and leaned back in her chair, rubbed her face in her hands. The investigation was going nowhere.

The phone rang and she hesitated, afraid it could be more bad news.

'Sheriff Nash,' she said into the mouthpiece.

'This is Captain Chris Slater, out in Denver. One of my men,

Detective Gavin Phillips, told me that you're looking for Will Bradley.'

'Hello, Captain,' Louise greeted him. 'That's right. I was expecting his call yesterday, but he never got back to me with an address or number.'

'My fault. I told Phillips to leave it with me, but we had some trouble out here and I didn't have a chance to get back to you.'

'What have you got for me?' she asked.

'Well, I served with Will for several years, back when we were both detectives working homicide. I've never seen a cop with the heart and soul Will had; a willingness to believe that no matter what rotten, sickening acts we experience, there is always a decent side to humanity. We had some good times back then. Hard times, too – but all my memories of Will are of a man who would give more than he took, make a stand for truth and justice . . . I figure if he wanted to keep in touch with any part of his past, I would be near the top of his list. But I haven't heard shit in fifteen years. He just disappeared. Vanished. And I think he likes it that way.'

'Do you have any idea at all regarding his location?' Louise asked. 'This is important.'

'There were a few rumours that he was heading for the West Coast – LA, San Francisco – somewhere nice. But that was a long time ago, and he could have moved on any number of times.'

'What happened to him?' Louise said, her curiosity piqued. If these two had gotten along so well, why did Bradley suddenly need to check out of reality?

'There was a guy named Dominick Rain. Real bad dude from these parts. They ended up shipping him to a criminal asylum near Los Angeles. He used to get his kicks by killing blind ladies. Young, old – it didn't make no difference to him.'

'That's disgusting.' Louise swallowed deeply.

'He used to torture them. Called it playing a game, messing with the senses they did have.' Slater paused. 'He used to . . . Well, you use your imagination, Sheriff Nash, if you ever care to ponder the subject. These were innocent women who wouldn't harm anybody. And he did nasty things to them.'

'Isn't that a little dramatic, Captain Slater?'

153

'You're a small-town cop, with small-town ways. No offence meant.'

'None taken.'

'What we saw would shock you. I've never seen anything like what we dealt with back then. People die, but what he used to do ... Out here, in any city I suspect, your skin gets a little thicker, wears a protective sheen, but even a lot of us city boys were shocked by what Dominick Rain did.'

'What has this to do with Will Bradley?'

'Will used to handle things a little differently. He cared for the dead, didn't talk of them as losers, but victims of a society slowly going mad. He looked into the eyes of every single body he saw, and I know he wanted to bring them back, that he was wishing for a way to save them. He never let go of his humanity. He would sometimes walk on a scene and puke like a rookie. He would talk with relatives and not just act as a cypher for their emotions. Actually communicate with them. And then Faith Gallagher came into his life ... Do you know who Faith Gallagher is?'

'She lives out here. The reason I wanted to talk with Will is because she has come forward to help us with a case. I was after a little advice on how to handle the situation.'

'Faith is a good woman, Sheriff Nash. You believe everything she tells you. Don't ever doubt her,' Slater said, before continuing: 'Dominick Rain had taken three lives that we knew of. We didn't know who he was then, just that some serial nut had started killing blind women. It turned out – or so he confessed at his trial – that there were four dead. Faith just walked into the department one day and insisted on speaking with a detective.'

Much as she had done here, Louise reflected, listening.

'We figured that maybe she thought somebody was following her, or that she was hearing noises at night. We were getting calls from a lot of very scared women. Could be a break. Then again it could just be a blind chick imagining things and getting spooked. We flipped a coin and it came up heads. Will won, but ... I don't know. He went to talk with her anyway. There was something in his eyes. I think, even then, he was falling in love with this woman he didn't even know.

'Will worked closely with Faith, who was a great help to us, and somewhere along the way they fell in love. One night after a long chase, we finally caught the guy, had him cornered. I shot him and his body fell into a river, washed away and was never recovered. Dominick Rain was dead. It was over. Everybody lived happily ever after. Except . . .' Slater hesitated.

'Go on,' Louise urged.

'The courtship of Will and Faith was always slow, conducted with trepidation, neither knowing how to handle or talk to the other. I don't even know if they ever slept together. But I do believe that in the short time they had together, they managed to love a lifetime's worth.'

'What went wrong?'

'Dominick Rain set us up. He must have waited downriver and recovered the body we presumed to be his. Buried it in an unmarked grave. Will always believed that with Faith's aid there would be opportunities to save those destined to die. He didn't realise that she would be the first.'

Louise tried to digest his words as he flipped from one scenario to another.

'Rain attacked Faith Gallagher at the Radford & Doyle Institute, knowing that he would never be safe as long as we had our blind witness. Will always blamed himself for that assault. He was there at the Institute, you see. He saved her, but not before . . .'

'Before what?' Louise pushed.

'Rain assaulted her. Touched her with his hand – all but raped her. Can you imagine that – how she must have felt? Will arrived, chased Rain. He saved her life. Almost killed Rain. Stabbed him with a screwdriver, if you can fucking believe that. He was ready to kill him, all right.'

Louise remained silent as Captain Slater recovered his emotions before continuing.

'Faith shut everybody out, including Will. She wouldn't talk to anybody. The fact that she wouldn't let Will near her hurt him. You see, in the beginning they had trouble communicating with each other. She was blind and that was hard for him to deal with, and she had never had a boyfriend in her life, didn't know what to do for him. It was slow and difficult, with a lot of treading on each

155

other's toes. But they did love each other, and Will was certain that they were close to finally getting it together. So when Faith wouldn't talk to him, or even see him, he didn't know how to react.'

Louise swallowed.

'It destroyed his humanity. He lost his edge. He waited and waited, but she wouldn't even return his calls. She just sat in the Institute in her room and refused to come out. Will became a shadow of the man he once was. He fell into a dark place; didn't care about anybody or anything.' Slater sighed heavily.

'By the time Faith came around, wanted to make contact with him and try again, Will had already left. Nothing I said could keep him here any longer. He would go to the Institute and sit outside her room, but she would never answer his knocks. He would tell her he was there and wait until sunrise, but she would never let him in. Until it was too late. And he was no longer waiting.'

This was nothing like the television movie, Louise thought. They never mentioned the love affair between Faith and Will Bradley, never told of their devastating loss. She was shown in a sympathetic light, but he had been depicted as a stereotype macho cop. It was very sad, and Louise was still holding out for a happy ending. She waited, silent, but realised Slater had nothing else to say.

'What about Rain?' she asked, pursuing another avenue.

'They should have juiced him, but his lawyers played up the fact that his past was quite tragic. I don't remember the details, but his childhood was all fucked up. Last I heard, he was still locked away. Listen, Will's a good man. If you ever get in touch with him, give him a break. He has a good heart.'

'Thanks for the talk, Captain Slater.'

'Anytime. What's happening out there?'

'Double murder. You homebred city boys might get used to staring hard crime down all the time, but here in Cradle violent offences are not a daily occurrence. On top of that, half my department is at home in bed with some freak flu. The FBI are sending somebody, but the cavalry hasn't arrived yet.'

'Well, you have some good luck out there, Sheriff Nash,' Slater concluded supportively.

Finding Madeline

Mike Castle arrived at the home of Madeline Crowe less than ten minutes after the call from Nadine telling him she was there. He had seen Roy Rogers and Trigger in town, Ennio Morricone's distinctive soundtrack to *The Good, The Bad and The Ugly* blasting from their vehicle. He needed her money in case they caught up with him. Madeline was either going to help him out, or he was going to get the hell out of Dodge before his head got broken.

His beat-up Chevy skidded to a halt, bouncing into the kerb. He jumped out and ran through the expansive garden to the front door. He knocked on it and was surprised when it eased open.

'Madeline!' Mike called urgently. 'You in here?'

He stepped cautiously inside, hoping her volatile husband wasn't home. He didn't want a conflict.

'Madeline, honey?'

'I'm in the . . . bedroom.'

Her voice sounded weak.

'What's wrong?' he called, taking the stairs two at a time. 'I'm coming up.'

'Please . . .'

He found her in a large bedroom, the second room he tried. He stopped dead in his tracks.

'My God,' he gasped. 'What did he do to you?'

Visiting Faith

When it rains, it sure does pour, Louise thought morosely, hanging up the telephone.

'Your timing's real good, Agent Ramsey,' she told the suited man who had introduced himself seconds ago, before the call had interrupted him. Dominick Rain smiled in response. She had barely glanced at his ID. However good or bad, the quality of Donald Blythe's work had been inconsequential. The telephone call had saved him any worry. 'Hicks! Come in here,' she called.

Introductions dispensed with, Louise continued: 'You and Deputy Hobson are going to have to go by the Crowe place by yourselves. Don't tell her about Russell yet. I've called Dr Bale and he'll meet you at the scene.'

'The scene?' Rain asked. 'I feel like I've arrived halfway through the plot. What's going on?'

Hicks left.

'The wife of Russell Crowe just called. She thought she heard something. Thinks there might be an intruder in the house.'

'Why the doctor?'

'Rumours spread quickly here, Ramsey. If word of her husband's death did get out last night, it might have reached Madeline by now. She could be in shock, jumping at shadows. Come on,' Louise said, grabbing her jacket.

'Where are we going?' Rain asked, following her out to the Maverick.

'To see Faith Gallagher.'

'The blind woman,' Rain whispered with a discreet smile.

'That's right,' Louise said. She turned the Maverick around and raced down Main Street. In her mirror she watched Hicks and Hobson turning out of view. 'A young biker called Albert

158

Dreyfuss helps to look after her. This morning he found her trussed up in her room. Somebody threatened her in the night.'

Threatened, Dominick Rain mused, staring out at the blurred desert landscape. Hues of red and orange and brown merged beneath the mountain ranges on the distant horizon, their peaks shrouded by low cloud. Whoever had attacked Faith Gallagher would have to pay with his life. No way will you steal my revenge, he thought viciously. It has kept me alive all these years in prison and then in the asylum with the crazy people. He wouldn't allow it to be taken from him now that he was so close.

He fixed his eyes on a point on the horizon, and resumed the persona of the dead FBI Agent Jack Ramsey trying to subdue his anger.

He could feel nothing except hatred and the throbbing desire to make the blind bitch suffer.

The urge to play the game was once again overwhelming him. He didn't know if he could control it, wondered for a second if he could keep his promise to Lorna, that they would live a normal life once this night was over . . .

Dominick studied the woman driving the Maverick. Sheriff Nash was young, in her early thirties, and attractive. Her overbite would be cute in more frivolous circumstances.

She glanced at him and laughed nervously. 'I got rhubarb growing out of my ear, or something?'

'Is that where we're heading?' Rain asked, pointing to a large house on the horizon, comfortable that he had easily won her over.

Louise nodded. 'Ms Gallagher lives out here by herself. Likes her own company. But she's a nice woman. You ever hear of her?'

Rain nodded slowly. 'I think I saw a movie once.'

'Well, she doesn't like the celebrity of it all. Once she helped to solve some big murders out in Denver. Some sick bastard was killing blind women.'

Dominick nodded, even managed to smile. Thought about what he was going to do to Faith Gallagher, and anybody who dared to get into his way.

* * *

'You must be Albert Dreyfuss. I'm Agent Jack Ramsey with the FBI,' Rain told the young man who answered the door.

Albert nodded. 'Come in. Hi, Sheriff Nash.'

'Hello, Albert. Where's Faith?' Louise asked, instantly taking charge. Regardless of who was here to help with the investigation, and how long she intended sticking around, this was still her job, her town, and she wouldn't have Faith questioned – perhaps even harassed – by an anonymous stranger.

They walked into the spacious living room.

'Louise, is that you?' Faith smiled, beginning to stand.

'Morning, Faith. Don't get up,' Louise told her, eased her back into the chair.

'You normally complain at me if I do anything like that,' Albert objected.

'Stop whining, Albert. Did I complain this morning when you untied those knots? Sometimes I don't mind accepting all the help I can get. Especially when I've been hit on the head.'

'The FBI has sent reinforcements. This is Agent Jack Ramsey,' Louise explained.

Dominick Rain moved forward and Faith flinched slightly as he leaned towards her. Something about him, just for a second . . . And then it was gone. Not a memory or a feeling. A reminder of the bad things that had happened. An old scent . . .

Dominick thought about wrapping his strong hands about her frail neck, crushing it.

Suddenly, without warning, one of Faith's hands reached up to touch his face. Lost in the dream, Dominick recoiled. He wanted to pull away as her fingers explored his features, but knew that would draw suspicion to himself. He wondered if she suspected anything, if she was searching him out with her psychic powers – the true him, looking deep inside his heart of darkness.

He didn't know how her power worked, whether she could use it to detect his true identity. All he could do was throw up a defence, a wall of meaningless thought that she would have to break through. Make no sense at all.

But he still began to perspire. She had moved away slightly when he had leaned close to her. *She knew something about him.*

He was suddenly absolutely certain that they were all looking at him, that they all knew the truth about who he was and all he had done in his life. He had to get out of here. Kill her and flee. *Kill them all.*

Dominick reached inside his jacket, felt the gun in the holster. Faith let go of his face.

Dominick removed his hand, relaxing. All she wanted to do, he thought, was put a face to his name.

'I hope you look better than you feel,' Faith joked, wondering for a brief moment about the scars on his face. Had he been wounded in the line of duty? Or perhaps it was something less heroic.

They all laughed at the comment.

Dominick wanted to be away from Faith Gallagher, away from this house. Being around her was no fun unless she knew his name and he could see her blind fear. Taste it. Hours now, he thought.

'Do you like gum?' Faith asked the agent.

The question surprised him, and then he realised what had happened. She had smelled his breath. The mint . . .

'Sometimes,' he responded. 'You want a stick?'

'No,' she whispered. 'For a second I thought I could smell mint on your breath. It reminded me of . . .'

Tabitha Warner. Pinned down. His breath on her face as he taunted the blind girl. Cut deep into her firm young flesh.

She remembers, Dominick thought. The game has already started. She thought it was done with when I went to prison, but *here I am again.*

It was stupid to still be chewing the mint gum – a habit he had never been able to break. It kept his mouth and breath feeling fresh. Clean. Everything always had to be clean.

'No, it reminded me of nothing,' Faith concluded, dismissing the horrific flash of memory.

'OK, then. Let's get the wagon on the road,' Louise said, sensing some kind of tension between her blind friend and the FBI agent she had only met this morning. 'What can you remember about last night?'

Arrest

Madeline was sitting on the edge of the bed. Her pretty features were not marked, but her arms were bleeding badly. There was a knife on the floor, the tip of the blade red. She quickly covered her breasts with her arms when Mike entered the room, but not before he noticed another cut on her stomach.

'Madeline!' Mike gasped.

She wrapped herself in the bedsheets. He reached out to her.

'Please . . . don't . . .' she sobbed, and retreated up the bed, away from him.

'What happened?' Mike asked, standing still and not daring to move in case he panicked her even more. 'Who did this to you?'

'Keep away!'

She reached down for the knife, brandished it tightly in his direction. She needed to be holding the knife in a gesture of defence when the police arrived, so that there was a reason for her prints to be all over it. The police would never doubt her explanation that Mike Castle had raped her at knifepoint after threatening to shoot her. After all, his prints were all over the handgun at the side of the bed. Nadine had made sure of that. Madeline had used her finger to place traces of his semen within her, obtained from the used condom Nadine had given to her.

She had taken care not to make the cuts too deep. Christ, it had hurt pulling that blade across herself. But the wounds were superficial and would not scar.

'Stay back,' she snarled. 'The police are coming.'

Mike moved slowly forward.

And that was when Deputy Dwayne Hicks and Deputy Claire Hobson burst into the room and saw him advancing on her.

'Freeze!' Hicks screamed.

Mike jumped, almost hit the ceiling. He turned and thrust his hands into the air. Hicks moved across the room and pushed his gun into the man's face.

'On the floor! Get down!'

'But—'

'Now!'

Mike quickly complied, dropping to his knees. He turned to Madeline, held out his hand. 'Madeline, honey. Tell them—'

'Don't let him near me!' Madeline panicked, scrambling away.

She nearly fell out of the far side of the bed, but Claire had moved over to comfort her and prevented her fall. She carefully eased the knife from the hysterical woman's hands.

'Come on,' Claire said gently. 'Let's get you out of here.'

'Madeline, please!' Mike exclaimed.

Hicks punched the man on the jaw. 'Shut up! Hands on the back of your head!'

Mike did as he was instructed, watching the two women shuffling from the room. He didn't understand what was happening, but didn't need telling twice as the cop's fist shot out again.

Perfume

Faith described her vision of the little girl. Louise queried what her connection might be with the murders. Was she a witness, perhaps? But what would a little girl be doing out at DP3 so late?

Louise thought it strange that the FBI agent appeared so unsceptical of Faith's powers. He seemed to believe her ability at face value and on word of mouth alone. Didn't need convincing.

Then Faith described being dragged out of bed, gagged and tied. Threatened.

'The man spoke several times. He told me to shut up and listen to what he had to say. He said . . .' Faith paused. His exact words had been: *'You be a good little girl and stop snooping.'*

'Do you think you might have been the little girl in the vision?' Louise asked immediately. It was obvious Faith was considering the same thing. 'It could have been an advance warning of the attack.'

'Are there any clues in the vision?' Dominick interrupted, performing his masquerade. 'Something that might hint the girl is you?'

He was concerned that if she *was* the little girl in the vision, and that it was a warning, then perhaps it was about his presence and not the threats from last night. He had to act fast and get out of Cradle.

'No. It's drained of colour. The actual image is sepia-toned. The sound crackles.' Faith managed a small laugh. 'The quality of the vision is very poor. Degraded. It looks like an old home movie.'

'Did you have anything like that in your family?' Louise asked. 'It could be a memory.'

'Or a coincidence,' Rain added flatly. He couldn't have Sheriff Nash believing Faith was in any kind of danger or she would put

164

a watch on the house. Naturally, if she did make such a decision, he would volunteer for the duty. Nash had already informed him of the current internal politics affecting her department – the reason there were only a couple of deputies working with her. She'd spoken of a mysterious flu virus that chose its victims selectively; anybody wearing a police uniform and not supporting their local sheriff was susceptible.

If he could be assigned as her bodyguard . . . Dominick smiled, picturing her fear as he removed his mask and revealed his true identity.

Louise looked at him sternly for his suggestion that Faith might be leading them all down the Yellow Brick Road. Maybe he didn't believe, she thought. The blind woman put a hand on her leg. Louise's muscles were tense.

'Don't worry, dear. I think he could be right.'

'What do you mean?' Louise asked, still staring at the FBI agent. He had no right to shoot his mouth off like that.

'I think it might be a coincidence. In the past I have had visions I have never understood, seen things that have never seemed relevant. I think this might have been one of those times,' Faith explained. Then she added thoughtfully, 'When Albert arrived this morning he was wearing too much aftershave. He does that sometimes. He's still a kid and doesn't know not to bath in it,' she smiled tenderly at him.

'What does this have to do with last night?' Rain asked bluntly.

'I suddenly realised what had been troubling me since the attack. The man who did it wasn't wearing aftershave. I don't even think he was a man.'

'What?' Louise gasped.

'*She* was wearing perfume. The person here last night was a woman. It was a very flowery aroma, like a summer garden blossoming. Very feminine. It was the same type you were wearing last night, Louise, when you came to tell me about the pills you had found near the fan.'

'Perfume?' Louise was stunned.

'Think about it,' Faith encouraged. 'Not only that, but her long nails cut my cheek when she slapped me.'

'That could have been a ring,' Louise suggested.

165

'Albert, do you still have the original swabs you used to clean the wound with?' Rain asked, playing detective.

'I left them in the bathroom. Why?'

'Could you get them for me? We can have them analysed and might find trace evidence. If it was a woman, I'm thinking we might find chips of nail varnish.'

Albert hurried out of the room, keen to be part of the detection process that was enthralling him.

'Also,' Faith continued, 'the pitch of her voice changed wildly, as though she was trying to disguise it. Not because I knew her; but to confuse me – to make me believe I was being attacked by a man. It was deeper, thicker. More resonant. However, when she called me a little girl her voice lost its vicious edge. She sounded just like a mother, chastising her children. *You be a good little girl and stop snooping.*'

Drawing In The Desert

That same morning Will Bradley had found Cradle and was parked in the desert about half a mile from Faith's cabin, wondering how he was ever going to approach her after all these years. Hearing a vehicle approach, he picked up his binoculars and watched a Maverick draw up outside her home. Interested in the visitors – a man and a woman – he adjusted his binoculars to get a better view. He had put down his sketch pad, the pages adorned with various renderings of the blind woman he loved.

A kid had already arrived, riding out of the hills on a scrambler. There was nothing out there except rocky desert and for a few minutes Will had pondered where the teenager had come from. He had been able to make out some caves through his binoculars, but figured he was too young to be some kind of wildman. There were signs of a campfire, bits of junk lying around.

That was about half an hour ago. Now the new people went inside.

The woman was wearing a sheriff's uniform, the man a dark suit. Will sat up, curious. He thought Faith had turned her back on the bad times, but what if she was involved here, pursuing some dark avenue that could only lead to hearts rotted by evil? What if she needed his help?

What was going on down there?

Will was stuck on a threshold. He wanted so badly to see her, but what could he say? *Long time, no see. How's it going?* He shook his head, beginning to sketch again. The woman who had climbed from the Maverick, and then the guy. All the time thinking that it was the same lack of self-confidence that had prevented him from going into her room all those years ago. He was making the same mistake again.

167

He shook his head. Did it matter what he said? They would be reunited. She would either like that, or not. He would either be with her for the rest of time, or never see her again.

He had ruined things back then, before the devastation, and now he was screwing up all over again. He wished Mitchell Ford had come with him from LA. His friend would have sorted his head out, dragged him kicking and screaming into the house, if necessary. What had Mitchell said before he left the city to come here?

You guys have got some horrible, long-distance Sleepless in Seattle *thing going. Only instead of jokes, you have dead bodies littered throughout the relationship.*

He'd come so far, and now he only had to take one last step.

But he couldn't move. Not until the people had left.

He gritted his teeth, pencil scribbling madly. That was only an excuse and he knew it; especially when they did leave and he continued to draw in the desert. The kid's still inside, he prevaricated. Let the kid leave and then I'll go see her . . . Or find another excuse to remain out here.

He watched the Sheriff climb into the Maverick. The man, who definitely looked like some kind of federal agent, walked around to the passenger side. He checked his sketches. Pretty accurate. What were they doing, talking to Faith? Studying them, he realised something wasn't quite right with the man. It was the suit: slightly long in the legs, a touch too short in the sleeves. It was barely noticeable, but from experience he knew those FBI guys were sharp-dressed men.

He studied his sketch of the man. There was something about him. Those scars . . . He began to work on the drawing, making subtle changes, eliminating those curious scars. Shading the lines and fleshing them out.

And then he looked down at who he had drawn; stared with horror at the face smiling back at him.

He forgot all about the kid leaving.

He grabbed his binoculars, could still see the Maverick, an ant nearing the small town. He got to his feet and ran to his car. He had to speak with the Sheriff. That was no federal agent in the vehicle with her!

The Truth According To Madeline

It was late morning when Louise and the FBI agent started back to town from Faith's home, and a call came over the radio from Deputy Dwayne Hicks.

'We just heard from Dr Bale over at the hospital. He found traces of semen when he examined Madeline Crowe. Fullton's already run some tests. Results show it's from that creep Castle we found at her place.'

'God,' Louise whispered, rubbing her face. What was happening here?

Dominick Rain listened. This Castle must be the same guy who had dared to harm Faith Gallagher before he himself could get to her. The man had signed his own death warrant.

'And that's not all, Louise. We found a gun at the scene,' Hicks informed them. 'His prints are all over it. It's the right type of weapon, so we're just waiting for Wade and Fullton to give us a match on the bullets they dug out of Russell Crowe's body.'

Louise was silent for a moment. 'If we had a confession,' she observed, 'even a motive, then this whole ballgame would be won.'

'A lot of the time,' Rain put forth, 'we don't know why a person does what he does. We have all the facts and evidence God can give us, but sometimes we never know why. The case is still closed once the bad guy is behind bars.'

'He killed Madeline's husband and raped her at gunpoint,' Hicks chimed in over the radio. 'Sick bastard.'

'But why?' Louise countered. 'He didn't have to kill her husband to rape her. Russell Crowe wasn't even supposed to be in town. He should have been at a conference . . . that's why nobody missed him. If he wasn't going to be in town, at home, why kill him?'

'Maybe Crowe did try to tell the man that. *I'm not even going to*

169

be in town. Let me live and you can keep the wife as long as you like.'

'Nice attitude, Hicks. You've been hanging out with Kenny again, haven't you?'

'What does the slimeball in lock-up have to say?' Rain asked, interrupting the small-town banter.

'The man – his name is Mike Castle, a reporter of no repute – claims he has been conducting a long-time affair with our very own Madeline Crowe. He says she was going to run out on her marriage – that's right, leave the rich guy – to live happily ever after with him.'

'You're joking!' Louise gasped.

'Uh huh. According to Castle, she was supposed to meet him at some motel out of town two nights ago. She never showed so he came to Cradle looking for her. He can give us dates when they met, but it was always in secret.'

'So there are no witnesses to the affair,' Rain presumed quietly.

'That's true,' Hicks agreed. 'But we don't need them.'

'Hicks, I know you like playing detective,' Louise told him, 'but please will you quit stalling and cut to the chase.'

'Remember Nadine Sherman? The woman you went out to Circle of Life with?'

'Sure, I know Nadine.' Don't let this be, Louise prayed. She already suspected her friend was somehow involved in the attack on Faith Gallagher. The Sheriff had borrowed the perfume that Faith recalled from Nadine's locker. And Albert had told them that he had seen a battered station wagon on the road into town last night, with a woman at the wheel who looked real upset. Nadine owned a vehicle of that description.

'Mike Castle claims that Nadine Sherman has knowledge of the affair,' Hicks related. 'He believes Madeline Crowe confides in her.'

'Well, that's possible. They used to be friends back in high school, and she approached her husband to get Nadine the job with Circle of Life. I'll talk with Nadine later.'

'There's no need,' Hicks told her.

'What are you, Hicks?'

'Mostly human.'

'I mean, are you clairvoyant? We need to confirm what these

people are saying. People can't just knock off a guy in my neighbour-hood and get away with it by telling whatever lies they like.'

'Louise, Madeline Crowe confirms that she did have an affair with Castle.'

'What?' Louise blurted, wondering if Faith's other vision, of a man falling from high castle walls, could have anything to do with Mike Castle. Was he somehow involved in this from the very beginning?

'The victim agrees they used to sleep together.'

'But not last night?' Rain asked.

'It's not that easy. Madeline says the affair was going on for about six months. It began as a one-night stand, but they met again, and then she didn't know how to stop it. When he started talking about marriage and her getting a divorce, she knew she had to pull the plug.'

'Do me a favour, Hicks? Put all this into one simple, linear report and have it ready for me at the end of the day. Could you do that for me?' Louise asked.

'She gave the affair the red light and that's when he came out here, looking for her. Looking for trouble,' Hicks ploughed on.

'We don't know he did anything yet,' Dominick Rain said.

'Come on, man. He raped her. He virtually had the gun in his hand when we busted in there. That weapon is going to prove he killed her husband.'

'We never saw him pull the trigger,' Louise stated.

'But we have his fingerprints all over it,' Hicks protested.

'Why did she sleep with Castle in the first place?' Louise asked.

Hicks hesitated, and the line crackled. 'Russell Crowe used to knock her about a little. She was afraid of her own husband and needed somebody to turn to. Knew that as he was the town saviour, nobody would listen to her here, so she found solace elsewhere. Come on, Louise! Madeline was your friend. Show a little compassion here. First her husband. Now this.'

'Small-town secrets,' Dominick whispered, really getting into his role. 'The ugly truth behind all those Norman Rockwell paintings and little white picket fences. I think there could be more here than Hicks believes.'

'Oh, lord,' Louise said sorrowfully. If Mike Castle had dumped the body of Russell Crowe in Lover's Lake, what was the connection with Ricky Turner? 'What is Castle wearing?'

'I don't know. Jeans and a shirt. We found a bag of clothes in his motel room. Same shit. Why?'

It didn't add up, Louise thought. His clothes simply wouldn't match the fibres Bobby Fullton had found under the nails of the dead kid, Ricky Turner. Perhaps Castle had been working with somebody. A woman . . . Madeline? *Russell Crowe used to knock her about a little.*

'Who told Madeline her husband had been murdered?'

Hicks paused. 'I don't know. She was hysterical at the hospital. Claire said she just blurted it out. It was probably Castle torturing her before he . . . did what he did. I mean, this guy is nutso. Do you want to know what else he claims?'

I don't believe Madeline actually helped to kill her own husband, Louise thought. This woman is my friend. She can't have done this.

'Go on,' she urged.

'He claims that Nadine Sherman came to his motel room last night, seduced him and then – get this – took the condom they used with her as some kind of souvenir. The guy is looney tunes!'

'That does sound pretty insane,' Rain observed.

'OK, Hicks. Get that report written. I'll be back at the office soon.' Louise cut the connection.

'I don't know,' Rain mused a minute later. 'Either this case is closed and I'm going home, or a whole lot of skeletons are going to tumble from somebody's closet.'

'I want you to stay around for a few days until we finish this.'

Dominick nodded, smiling pleasantly. 'Not a problem.'

'In a minute I'll drop you somewhere good to get lunch,' Louise told him. 'Then I have to visit a friend.'

'Nadine Sherman?'

Louise nodded. 'I think . . . never mind.' *I think she might be in a lot of trouble.*

'You want me to come?' Rain asked, sensing her mood.

'No. Thanks, but I think it will be easier for her to talk if I visit her alone.'

172

Hysteria

Nadine, Louise thought when she parked in front of her friend's house. Somehow she was involved in all this mess. Louise had to see her, talk with her. She couldn't convict a person just because they liked a certain brand of perfume, but she had a really bad feeling ripping into her gut. *Soul-mates.* I have to help her if I can, she thought.

Nadine had wanted to have a serious conversation for days, had something big on her mind. She'd tried to talk about it on the way to Circle of Life, and then again in the locker room after Louise had been down Drain Pipe Three.

But the words weren't coming out right. Louise was listening, but not hearing what she was supposed to hear. Which was what – a cry for help? *What were you trying to tell me, Nadine?*

More than ever Louise felt she needed to know the identity of Nadine's secret visitor, the morning she hadn't been invited in, prior to their visit to Circle of Life. That was when she had first noticed the preoccupation, the change in her friend's mood.

As she climbed from the Maverick, a car skidded to a jagged halt next to it, bouncing up the kerb.

Louise removed her sunglasses as the man climbed out.

'Do you actually own a driving licence?' Louise asked the driver sternly, shaking her head.

'Sheriff,' the man began urgently, 'you have to listen to me!'

'I'm a little busy right now. Go down to the department and tell them I busted you for reckless driving. Alternatively, explain to *them* what is so important that you had to nearly run me down.'

He grabbed the front of her jacket, and she shrugged away, hand falling to her sidearm.

'You have to look at these!' he pleaded, reaching into the car

173

and pulling out a sheaf of illustrations. He waved the pages in her face. 'This is an emergency!'

Fifteen minutes later, Louise Nash and Will Bradley were still arguing heatedly at the side of the road. Although Louise was delighted to meet the man she'd heard so much about, there was no way she was going to swallow his outlandish story. It was straight out of an Alfred Hitchcock movie.

'Will, Dominick Rain is still in prison,' she said patiently. 'I spoke with your old friend Chris Slater earlier. He said Rain hasn't seen the light of day for fifteen years or more.'

'It's him, all right. I'll never forget his face!' Will snarled. 'He has come to Cradle to kill Faith Gallagher, and you're going to sit back and let him do it.'

'Please, Will,' Louise implored, holding his arm. 'Faith loves you. She misses you. Go see her. If it makes you feel better, watch over her. But please – go and talk to her.'

'And say what? Sorry I'm fifteen years too late. After all I did that just doesn't make the grade.'

Louise sensed his hysteria was dying and slowly began to walk him to his car.

'She doesn't blame you, Will. I'm the Sheriff of Cradle – for now – and somewhere along the way it became a bad place. People are dying here, my friend, but it has nothing to do with Agent Jack Ramsey. Please stay away from him.'

'I can't promise you that,' Will told her, staring intently at his sketches. He knew who the agent really was. 'I should have killed him years ago.' This was his second chance.

'You didn't come here for that,' Louise reminded him. 'You came here for Faith.'

'Will you do one thing for me?' he asked the Sheriff.

'Anything, except shoot the Fed,' Louise smiled gently.

'Take a look at his chest and—'

'How am I supposed to do that?'

'You'll think of something. See if he has a scar – a real ugly one, a couple of inches long. You know what that means?'

Louise nodded. Bradley had tried to kill Dominick Rain with a screwdriver.

'I've got a better idea,' she said. 'Why don't I fax his office – have them send me a picture of what Ramsey is supposed to look like?'

'That works for me.' Bradley nodded, but his eyes remained sullen.

'Hey, I'm going to check into it – even if it means I have to rip his shirt off and examine his chest with a magnifying glass.'

Will Bradley did not laugh at her joke.

'I appreciate your help, Sheriff Nash, but I'm telling you for the last time who that man is, what his intentions are. His name is Dominick Rain, and he has come here to kill Faith Gallagher. But I won't let him hurt her again. He dies first.'

Nadine Sherman

'Come in,' Nadine told her friend solemnly, and they walked into the living room. 'I've been waiting for you. I'm glad you came alone.'

'Where are the children?'

'They're with Cutter. He's a friend from Circle of Life. I didn't want them to be here for this.'

'For what, Nadine?'

'I think you know. Please don't make me say it. If you hadn't come over here, I would have visited you.' *Or killed myself*, Nadine thought gloomily, remembering sitting in the bathtub earlier, the water cold, the knife on her wrist, trying . . . But staying alive for her children.

'Nadine, did you attack Faith Gallagher last night?' Louise asked, trying to remain devoid of emotion. Forget she's your friend and do the job.

Nadine fell into a chair and began to weep silently. 'So you came about that? You don't even know . . . I didn't mean to attack her.'

'Know what? Why did you go to her house last night? What's become of you, Nadine?' she asked, moving to hold her.

'She said she loved me,' Nadine wept. 'That if I helped her, the kids and I would have everything we ever needed. After Jimmy walked out and I got that crappy job . . . I thought it would be security for the future.'

'Who loved you?'

Nadine hesitated, but the time had come to unburden her soul. She couldn't live with the guilt any longer.

'Madeline Crowe. Her husband used to beat her, rough her up real bad.'

'Why didn't she come to see me?' Louise asked, sensing that Nadine was about to tell her everything.

'It's been going on for years. Once you got into the department, it was as though you had less time for your old friends. You were more career orientated and—'

'That's not true,' Louise protested, but she knew it was. 'I could have helped.'

'Madeline was so afraid of him. She was worried that if she did go to you and you tried to arrest him . . . What if he got out, or the prosecution failed? She asked me to help her, said she loved me.'

'Nadine, what have you done?'

Nadine began to sob harshly, her body trembling. 'We killed him, Louise. *I killed him.*'

Louise didn't know what to say as she held her shuddering friend. She thought Nadine had attacked Faith Gallagher, that she was all messed up for some reason, needed talking to and straightening out. But this . . . It was unbelievable.

'Will you help me?' Nadine pleaded.

Soul-mates for ever, Louise thought. God, what was she going to do? 'What happened?' she managed.

Nadine blew her nose and made a huge effort to gather herself. 'Madeline came to me one night. I was drunk and it was an easy seduction. I've always preferred women.'

The conversation in the Maverick, Louise thought, on the way out to Circle of Life.

'When we were kids I had such a crush on you,' Nadine confessed. 'I used to watch you in the showers after gym, walking to class . . . all the time. God, I can't believe I'm telling you all this. I thought maybe I was just attracted to women, but I've had some great times with guys. Even married one. With Madeline it was nice, but something didn't feel right. She never seemed a hundred per cent comfortable when she was with me, as though she was there because she had to be, not because she wanted to be. Louise, I think I love you. With you it would be—'

'Enough,' Louise interrupted softly, holding up her hand. 'We're friends, Nadine. Soul-mates, OK – but I love Wade Phelan. I'm sorry. I really am.'

Nadine nodded weakly. 'Madeline said she loved me, that she

always had. I didn't believe her, but I could see that she needed somebody.'

'Nadine, I think we should—'

'It was never about love. Greed and money – that was all. I needed the money for my children. Please don't take me away yet. Let me talk this through, then arrest me and do your thing. Oh God, what will happen to my children?' she cried.

'They'll be well looked after. But I don't have any answers.' Only more questions, she thought sadly, wondering if she would be able to arrest her friend. *Soul-mates*. 'What happened next?'

'I hated Russell for the way he treated her. She'd come to me, bruised and weeping. We both wanted to hurt him so badly . . . and then one night she told me she'd met somebody.'

'Mike Castle?' Louise asked.

Nadine nodded. 'How did you know?'

'We're holding him for raping Madeline. We suspected him of killing Russell.'

'He didn't do it!' Nadine cried. 'He didn't do any of it. Poor bastard. At first I was angry that she was sleeping around, but then she explained what she had in mind, and told me what would happen if Russell was murdered, about the money she would get. Castle was on some kind of medication and Madeline said she would leave some of his special pills wherever we decided to dump her husband's body. We would split the work down the middle. We tossed a coin.' Nadine began to laugh hysterically. 'Heads I would kill him and tails she would dispose of the body. That's how it went down.'

Louise let her friend cry through the next bout of tears. She was repulsed by what the two women had conspired to do together. A premeditated act, with poor Mike Castle to carry the blame.

'But then she told me about the kid. We were going to dump Russell's body in the lake, near the outflow from Drain Pipe Three, and she had gone up there wearing shoes that would fit Castle to leave some footprints. Ricky Turner was up near the rain-hole, injecting himself with drugs. A living, breathing, walking, talking pharmacy, Madeline told me. He probably thought he was hallucinating. Madeline said she teased him a little and then pushed him. She didn't tell me about him until after I had found the body at DP3. She said I wasn't to worry because nobody would suspect me after I had found the body.'

'What about killing her husband? How did you—?'

'I must have loathed him because I don't remember feeling anything when I pulled the trigger,' Nadine confessed.

Louise shook her head slowly. 'Help me to understand this, Nadine. How can you sit here and tell me these terrible things?'

'He was a womaniser, Louise. He used to hurt her. This whole thing is about seduction. Without my power, Mike Castle wouldn't be in jail. Without Madeline's, I wouldn't have fallen for her. In the set-up Madeline devised, I seduced Russell Crowe. We drove into the desert, out in a random direction, Russell and I. He just wanted us to be alone, where nobody would ever see us. Madeline followed in an old wreck and when I . . . had shot him, she picked up the body.'

'And then she dumped him into what was once Lover's Lake, and everything would have gone fine if I hadn't dredged it up. Jesus, Nadine, did you know he was still alive?'

'What?'

'He drowned. He survived the shooting. He can't have been in a pretty way, but he was still breathing.'

'Madeline never told me.'

Madeline probably enjoyed it, Louise thought. Got a kick out of the fact that her old man wasn't yet dead, that he was going to suffer a little more. It was suggested in the way she had killed the kid, breaking his fingers with her booted foot as he hung on for his life. Teasing him first, Nadine had just said.

Nadine was just another victim here. Yes, it was about seduction, all right. One that Madeline had probably planned for a long, long time so that she could get her husband's money.

She had even lured poor Mike Castle here to take the fall. The murder might have gone unsolved, but Madeline had wanted the certain knowledge that people would not come looking for her. That she would never be a suspect. An arrest and conviction would have secured that.

Louise wondered what Madeline had in mind for Nadine if their plan had succeeded. She was sure her friend would not have seen any of the money she so desperately wanted to provide her children with security.

'Louise, will you please hold me.'

Sheriff Nash reached for Nadine, hugged her, held her tight.

'Tell me everything will be all right.'

'I'm sorry. I can't do that, Nadine. I don't know if it will be.'

And they both cried in each other's arms, wishing for simpler times, the days of their happy childhoods when decisions were far easier to make and friends were for ever.

Mike Castle

Instead of getting lunch, Dominick Rain walked a couple of blocks to the almost deserted department building. This sly strike by most of Cradle's law enforcement certainly made life easy for lawbreakers, he reflected, although the mayor had called for an emergency town meeting to take place the following morning.

But for now the only occupants of the building were Deputy Dwayne Hicks, typing slowly before a computer monitor, and the doomed Mike Castle.

'You alone here?' Rain asked the young deputy.

Hicks looked up from the screen, startled. He nodded. 'You almost gave me a heart attack, Agent Ramsey. Deputy Hobson went for doughnuts.'

Rain smiled. Just three of them left – Hobson, Hicks and Nash – and they could still find time to eat doughnuts.

'Where's the prisoner?' he asked, moving around the desk, hoping he didn't sound too eager. 'I need to ask him some questions.'

'Castle's in the holding cell. It's in the back, there,' Hicks said, motioning to a corridor with his hand. He turned to the FBI agent. 'You want to wait a couple of minutes? I'm almost about ready to print out this damn thing.'

'What is it?'

'The report Louise asked for. This guy really is one sick puppy.'

'I'll need the keys,' Rain said, holding out his hand.

'You need the keys to question a man?' Hicks murmured quizzically, engrossed by the screen. 'Shit,' he whispered, making another error. At least it was an easy delete now instead of a form covered in white-out. The old sheriff used to chew his butt off so much for that. He was surprised he had any butt left to sit on. 'I don't know about that. You can't talk to him through the bars?'

'It's an FBI thing,' Rain said, suppressing the desire to kill the deputy. He was running out of time. Hobson would be returning soon with the doughnuts, and he didn't know how long Nash would be. If he had to, he would kill them all.

'They're in my jacket pocket,' Hicks mumbled absently, concentrating on the screen. 'Over there.'

Rain retrieved the keys and walked to the cage. He unlocked the barred door and entered the cell.

'How did it feel?' he asked the dishevelled hack, checking to make sure Hicks was out of earshot.

'I don't know what you're talking about,' Castle moaned, sitting up and moving to the edge of the bunk. At least he was safe from Roy Rogers and Trigger in here. 'Who the fuck are you, anyway?'

'I've only ever killed blind people myself,' Rain continued calmly, quietly, not concerned about his confession because Castle didn't have long to live. 'Why did you do it?'

'Are you fucking insane? Who the fuck are you? What the fuck do you want from me?' Castle said angrily, rising to his feet. 'I didn't do anything. I came to this town to . . . Oh, forget it. This whole fucking place is crazy!'

'I see,' Rain whispered. 'Maybe you are innocent.'

'So I keep telling them. Do you believe me?'

'You don't look like no cold-hearted killer. You don't really look like much. I don't know if you did what they say you did. I don't really care. But you shouldn't have messed with my woman.'

'What the fuck are you talking about? I didn't rape her!' Castle protested.

'I'm not bothered about that bitch in the hospital. I'm talking about Faith Gallagher,' Rain asserted. He removed his gun.

'Who? What are you doing?' Castle panicked. 'I don't even know who you're talking about.'

Rain sensed the man was about to cry out for help, so made the call for him as he brandished the weapon.

'Hicks! I could use a hand in here!'

Hicks had finished the report and wandered over to the printer. He heard the shout and turned. He was halfway to the cage when the three shots reverberated in his ears.

Darkness Falls

Heavy, low clouds rolled over the beautiful desert landscape, casting an eternal shadow over Cradle, bringing with them the night.

Louise and Wade were at her home preparing a salad together. Max was pacing the room impatiently, drooling for scraps. Occasionally one of them would throw him a sliver of meat to catch. Or drop.

Louise was lethargic after the day's activities, and was not looking forward to relieving Hobson and Hicks at ten. At the last minute, before leaving the department for this break, she had remembered to fax the Bureau for a photograph of Agent Jack Ramsey. She believed it was a fruitless exercise and had left before getting a response. However, she decided it might help Will Bradley through whatever psychological problems he had, and would show him the picture tomorrow.

She would watch the department through the night and then attend the town meeting. And then go to sleep for a long time and wake in a different town or city, far away from here. With Wade at her side.

After bringing Nadine in and discovering the mess Agent Ramsey had made of Mike Castle, when the innocent man had tried to escape, Louise had gone with the FBI man to talk with Madeline Crowe. They had made it obvious to the widow that she was a suspect in her husband's death and had left her at the hospital.

Madeline later tried to leave, but Dr Bale had insisted she stay in for observation through the night, and that was when Nadine had arrived to visit her.

Of course, Nadine was wearing a wire and it had not taken

183

long for Madeline to lose her cool and angrily implicate herself.

That was when Louise and Agent Ramsey had appeared in the doorway.

There had been no rape.

Mike Castle was innocent. And dead. *Dead!*

Louise felt terrible.

'I've known Nadine and Madeline since I was a kid,' she explained to Wade, who had only arrived an hour ago. She struggled to express her emotions and her voice cracked, like the lightning charging the atmosphere outside. 'Nadine since the day I was born.'

Soul-mates for ever.

Wade didn't have any answers for her. He cuddled her, urged her through the tears. On the other side of them he knew that although she wouldn't understand any more than she did now, at least she might feel better. A lot of repressed anger about the town poured out, released by sorrow for what had happened to her friends, what had become of them.

Tomorrow, at the town meeting, the whole issue of her being Sheriff would be resolved one way or another. And one way or another, she would still be leaving town once all the paperwork had been wrapped up. They could recall her for the courtcase, but she didn't want to remain here one day longer than she had to.

'I want to get out of here,' she told Wade when her tears began to dry. 'Can we do that?'

'Promise me one thing, honey. That you want to do this because you want to do it, not because you feel these people are trying to run you out of your job.'

'Wade, I hate this place and I want to find a new home . . . with you. Will you come with me, Wade?'

'You know I will,' Wade grinned.

'Will we still have the stars?'

'The stars will always be with us, Louise. They belong to us.'

And for an hour or so they forgot all about the meal they were preparing, forgot all about what had happened.

For that short time, she and Wade were the only people in the world. After making love they went to the bedroom and watched their stars. When the telephone rang, she made the mistake of picking it up. Deputies Hicks and Hobson had been called out to the Sunset Motel. She had no option but to go into the office.

The Lost Star

The drive to The Lost Star Tavern was a confusing one for Louise. She was now certain that Faith Gallagher was in danger, but also had a bad feeling that the call which had taken Deputies Hicks and Hobson all the way to the town's limits – in the opposite direction to Faith's home – might be bogus, a trap to get them out of the way.

The real Agent Ramsey, a likeness of whom she had found in a fax when she got to the deserted office, was undoubtedly dead and his impostor knew the political situation of the town which basically left her department in a dire position.

It occurred to her with a sense of dread that the Sunset Motel was the same one Agent Ramsey – *Dominick Rain*, she corrected – was staying at. She had tried calling them, but had gotten no response on the radio, figured they must have already reached the motel.

She had called Faith Gallagher from the department building, and ordered her not to let anybody in.

'What's wrong?' Faith asked. 'Is *he* here?' Her voice trembled.

Louise ignored the question. 'I'm on my way. I'll explain when I get out there. Under no circumstances, Faith. *Nobody.*'

Louise accelerated wildly through the stormy night landscape, racing through town, trying to avoid contemplating what Dominick Rain might be doing at this very minute to Faith Gallagher. With any luck Will Bradley would already be at her home. She thought too of Hicks and Hobson.

Dwayne Hicks had stood apart from his peers and backed her one hundred per cent, while Claire had been a bigger surprise, especially since she was sleeping with Kenny and usually worshipped his every word.

186

The Sheriff had tears in her eyes as she skidded into the busy parking lot of The Lost Star. Hobson had walked into her office yesterday . . .

I'm not your friend, Claire had told her bluntly, *but I don't believe what is happening in Cradle at the moment. I'm shamed by it. I put on this uniform, this badge, and wear it with pride. It says I'm willing to protect the people of this town, however divided they are. Kenny is good to me – I know you probably don't buy that – but on this one he's way wrong. We're the law. We can't just go on strike – you know that's all this is – because we don't like our new boss. If it had gone to a vote I doubt you would be standing behind that desk. But it didn't go to a vote. You were promoted and you are my Sheriff – I'll do what you ask, even if I don't like it or agree with it.*

Louise killed the engine, wiped at her eyes. Hicks and Hobson could take care of themselves, she thought, although they weren't trained to deal with serial killers intent on revenge. None of them were, except perhaps for Will Bradley – crusading for his own vengeance and a love that had never died – and she didn't know where he was.

Deputy Hicks and Deputy Hobson reached the motel just as Louise left the department building. They skidded to a halt, cutting the lights and siren.

'Which room did she say?' Hobson asked.

They both climbed from the car.

'Six,' he told her. 'Isn't this the motel Agent Ramsey is staying at?'

Thanks to the booming thunder, neither of them heard the first shot.

When Hobson didn't respond, Dwayne turned to her. She had fallen behind the car.

'Claire?' he asked, moving around the vehicle. Then he saw her on the ground, her hand clamped to a bloody wound on her thigh. He fell to his knees.

'Hobson!' he exclaimed. There was so much blood, gushing into the rain. It looked like a nasty wound, but not fatal. He applied pressure in an attempt to stop the bleeding, removed his jacket and covered her. He grabbed the radio from the car. 'I need help. I—' When nobody answered he realised the stark truth of their situation. There was nobody in the department building to send help. *They were all on strike.*

'Don't worry,' he whispered frantically to Hobson, looking around for the marksman. Spotting a tiny glint of light reflecting off a streetlamp – a telescopic sight – he pulled out his handgun and then he fell too, coming to rest next to Hobson.

Lorna climbed from her hiding place and put the rifle into the back of the car. Dominick had told her to kill the deputies, but she couldn't do that. She had wounded them and would call an ambulance on her way out of town.

There was only one person who needed to be killed, and that was Faith Gallagher. After that, she and Dominick could begin a normal life.

When the doorbell rang, Faith Gallagher was reaching into the fridge for a drink.

She thought about not answering as Sheriff Nash had instructed, but of course it might be Albert, or Louise herself. Maybe even Will, she thought hopefully. She made her way to the door, and opened it cautiously. Rain blew into her face.

'Who is it?'

Somebody mumbled, 'It's me. I'm soaked.'

'Albert?' She reached up, felt his face, identifying him by his features. He was cold and wet, his hair a straggly mess. 'You silly boy, you'll catch your death. Come in here.'

Dominick Rain smiled at the blood she had gotten on her hand. It looked slick. He carried Albert's head inside, blood dripping from the jagged neck-wound, and placed it on the side. She had been fooled so easily.

Earlier, Sheriff Nash had taken his handgun for testing, although she had told him there was no problem with his statement. It was standard operating procedure. He wasn't concerned with losing the gun. There were knives here, sharp blades with which he would hurt Faith Gallagher.

And then, while she was still breathing, he would slice out her eyes so that there would be no more visions.

So that she could never witness any more of his atrocities.

Louise had always hated The Lost Star Tavern. When she was a teenager, her friends – Nadine included – used to drag her down here, prowling for men. It was always full of drunken bums who would vomit down your dress as soon as romance you. Then they would expect you to sleep with them!

When she walked in, the doors swinging back behind her like saloon doors in an old Western, she saw that the scene hadn't changed much. The music was louder, the bums younger, that was all. And there were a lot more of them – mainly personnel from her department.

'I need help,' she began weakly, but nobody heard her.

Nobody even noticed her presence. They kept on dancing, drinking. Talking and shouting. Kissing. And she was glad, because the words had sounded fragile, like she was begging.

She focused on the old jukebox and fired two shots into its glass front, grateful that The Lost Star didn't have a live band performing. The music stopped suddenly. People came to a slow halt on the dance-floor and the conversation ceased.

'Hey!' the bartender protested.

'Never mind that,' she said icily, with a glare that made him freeze in his advancing tracks. 'People are in danger. Friends of ours. I need your help,' she said, searching for her deputies in the smoky atmosphere.

'Help?' somebody scoffed from the back. 'Isn't that your job?'

'Yeah!' another person jeered, a half-naked woman on the dance-floor, leaning in a stupor on her friend. 'Your people are supposed to protect us!'

'My people,' Louise began calmly, dismayed by the tension in the room, the hostility she felt against her. It had been a mistake to come here: she should have gone directly to Faith Gallagher's. She sighed. 'My people,' she declared, 'with few exceptions, are scum.'

A beer glass shattered on the wall behind her and she spun, gun raised. She hadn't come here to start a riot. Her hand was quaking and she spotted Kenny laughing. He had thrown the glass.

'Maybe,' the bartender sneered aggressively, 'if you give Kenny that shield pinned on your pretty little breast there, we can rustle up a small vigilante force to help him.'

Some of the Neanderthal men in the crowd began to whoop at the prospect of breaking out their home firearms.

'There'll be no vigilantes tonight,' she said, failing to silence them. She fired another shot, this time into the ceiling, and then holstered her weapon when they shut up. 'I'm talking to the deputies in this room. I need your help.'

Somewhere a ghettoblaster came on, with a heavy bass and screaming guitars. People began to dance and cheer. The bartender moved back behind the bar and resumed pouring drinks. Louise stood there for a moment and then realised they were just going to ignore her.

She turned and ran from The Lost Star, having wasted valuable time.

She wrenched the Maverick's steering wheel and raced back onto the road, heading for the desert.

Veronica Palmer had enjoyed her jog into the desert, but the hill up to Albert's cave was really killing her and when she had set out that evening she hadn't expected a goddamn storm to come rolling in. Now she was thoroughly soaked and was probably going to catch pneumonia. The wind was making the climb more difficult, but she was still looking forward to the prospect of sitting up all night with her new boyfriend. Her legs ached, and he could massage them for her, work his hands up . . .

As she breasted the hill, she saw a dark figure stagger out of Albert's cave.

Veronica slowed as the man bent over and . . . *puked*. God, he was vomiting all over the place. And where was Albert? He was supposed to be waiting here for her.

'Who's there?' she asked stridently.

The man stood upright, wiping his lip and chin. He was old – older, anyway – and heavily built. But she couldn't make out any details because of the night and the crappy weather.

'Do you know the kid that lives here?' the man asked, suddenly clicking on a torch and shining it in her face.

She stepped forward bravely, her legs quivering with trepidation and her long run. 'Yeah. He's my boyfriend. Who are you?'

'Listen to me carefully. What's your name?'

'Veronica Palmer. Who are you? And where's Albert?' she demanded, walking closer, edging around him. 'Albert?' she called, and then bolted for the cave.

The man moved fast for his size and scooped her lithe figure into his hands, pulling her back.

'Albert! Help me!' she cried, kicking and struggling, but unable to escape his tight grasp.

'Don't go in there,' the man cautioned. 'You can't go in there! Albert's . . . I'm sorry. But he's gone, Veronica.'

'What are you talking about? Let go of me!'

'Veronica, he's dead. I'm so sorry.'

The fight suddenly left Veronica; her body deflated.

'What?' she stammered. 'You killed him?'

'Do killers usually throw up after they've done their business?'

'How should I know? Who are you? I've got Mace.'

Veronica was facing him now, her body trembling with anger and confusion.

'I didn't kill him. I'm a police detective,' Will Bradley explained compassionately. 'I used to be . . . I came up here to ask Albert a few questions; I needed his help. I know you're upset, Veronica, but I need you to be strong. Can you do that? He . . . he hasn't been dead long and I think I know where the man who killed him is. I think he might be hurting somebody else.'

Veronica began to cry softly in the heavy rain.

'This is what you have to do. Take Albert's scrambler and go into town. Get Sheriff Nash and tell her what has happened. Tell her that Detective Bradley was right. She'll know what to do.'

'But what about you?' Veronica asked uncertainly.

'You'll drop me close to the home of Faith Gallagher,' Will told her.

'The blind lady?'

'Yes. The man who killed Albert wants her dead. If he hears the engine of the bike I think he will just murder her and get out. But if he doesn't know I'm coming he'll . . .' *Kill her slowly*, Will thought morosely. Torture her. He had found Albert in the cave,

191

decapitated. Dominick Rain was playing the game, wanted Faith to believe she was safe, in the company of a friend, before he pulled the blade of a cold knife across her throat.

She Who Can See

Faith turned, startled by Albert's sudden presence at her side.

'Albert, will you please try to call Louise Nash?' she asked, her heart pounding, suspecting that she was the little girl in the vision, that she was in grave danger. He didn't respond. 'Albert?'

He leaned closer. She could feel his breath on her face. The scent of mint . . .

'Albert's dead.'

'But—'

'That was just his head. I cut it off.'

'No!' Faith screamed.

'Do you know who I am?'

Suddenly the blade of a knife was making a shallow cut on her throat. She tried to get away, but he held her firmly in the chair.

'Rain,' she gasped. 'You are Dominick Rain.'

'I've come to kill you, blind woman. She who can see me, all I do.' Rain shoved her brutally onto the floor. 'Now run!' he ordered her, and laughed cruelly. 'We're going to play a game.'

The Endless Road

Louise couldn't think of Faith as she sped down the roads towards her home. Of what Dominick Rain might be doing to her even now . . . At first she thought of Nadine, but that didn't help. The other woman was part of the horrible situation she was facing. Friendships ruined. A serial killer loose in their small town. How could any of this be?

She nearly lost control of the Maverick and slowed a little, realising that if she crashed . . .

She wondered if she would ever see Wade again after tonight. She was scared and wanted to turn back and be with him, but knew that if she did Faith might die. That this was still her job, whether people liked her being Sheriff or not.

Forget everyone and everything for now, she told herself. Concentrate on surviving through this night. She accelerated, leaning heavily on the pedal. Rain might not even be there yet. If so, she would get Faith out, take her somewhere safe. Then wait for him.

Although forbidden, her thoughts went to Wade and what they would do when this was all over. They'd race to the horizon, into the painted desert to the point where the gorgeous sky touched the hard ground. It was an horizon they would never reach. Under their stars, they would travel an endless road together.

Hide And Seek

Faith fled the room, crying frantically, 'Lights out! Lights out!' as she careered from one item of furniture to another.

She couldn't remember which rooms were illuminated and she needed to plunge them all into darkness. Equal ground. It was her only chance. Dominick Rain wouldn't be able to undo her commands because the computer module would not recognise his voice.

'Run!' he called after her, roaring with laughter. 'Hide! I'm coming to get you!'

She stumbled, but kept on moving. His voice haunted her as she ran into the bedroom.

'Hide well, Faith, because when I find you, I'm going to kill you! Slowly!'

She caught herself painfully on the corner of the bed, and cursed the noise she was making. She had to stop this blind panic. She knew this house, was familiar with every inch. He was lost in dark territory. She could use that to her advantage.

She stood and tried to control her ragged breathing, listening for him. Her heart missed a beat at an explosion of sound. Just a door being kicked open. She heard him destroying the room, ripping it apart in his search for her. She wondered if it frustrated him that he couldn't find any light switches.

'Not in there, eh?' he declared. 'No matter. Soon I shall find you and then . . . I'll hold you to the floor, Faith. Pin you there and fuck your blind little cunt. Did you ever let Will touch you that way?' He sniggered demonically.

She whimpered involuntarily, put a hand over her mouth.

'Thought not,' he said in low tones, and she could hear him. He was close. 'I know where you are, Faith.'

195

She listened to his deliberately heavy walk in the hallway. He was pulling pictures off the wall, frames shattering. Albert had hung them for her. She thought of poor Albert, of his lifeless wet head, and a shudder convulsed her.

'That's just the beginning,' he sang out.

She swallowed deeply, biting her hand to stifle the screams which rose in her throat. She tasted her own blood. She was sure he was outside the room.

'I know you're in here,' he said. 'One, two, three. Coming in, ready or not.'

He kicked the door open and Faith clamped down on her hand, grinding the bone.

'Once I've had you – it will be nice, and very painful, my little psychic – I'm going to kill you. I intend to enjoy it. No interruptions like last time.'

Her eyes blinked open. He was in the next room, destroying it as he had the last. She wanted to run from the bedroom, but her feet were nailed to the floor. She could bolt past him, beyond his reach, out of the house and then sprint in any direction. He would never find her in the storm.

But she couldn't move. His voice held her still like a rabbit trapped in the headlights of a speeding vehicle.

'I'm going to bleed you dry, Faith. Slowly, drop by drop.'

And then he screamed, a primal cry of rage because he couldn't find her, a devastating turmoil in his heart.

She began to cry. Could hold the tears back no longer.

'I can hear you!'

He was stomping deliberately along the hall, knowing that his noise was a weapon with which to instil fear. The game was one of mind torture; a painful game he had endured all his childhood.

She tried to remain still in the dark, knowing that he would get the right room this time. Silent. She listened to her heart hammer, her breathing rasp. She tried not to sob or sniff.

'*I can see you,*' he hissed.

He was here, in the room, watching her. But it was pitch blackness, so how could that be?

It was part of his game, she thought. He was trying to provoke her into panicked, disorientated flight. So that she would fall and he would prey upon her like—

'You're beside the bed, next to the window. We're going to have so much fun now. Let's party, Faith.'

Next to the window . . .

'I'm going to find the fear in your eyes, Faith, and then dig them out so that you can never see me again.'

The shallow moonlight, fighting through broken clouds . . . Her silhouette against the night sky! A shadow, but enough. She heard him walking into the room, had to do something.

'Curtains close!' she blurted, dropping to the floor behind the large bed. The curtains rattled along the railings and she stealthily began to crawl under the bed.

'Hide and seek, eh?' he whispered harshly, tired of the chase now and annoyed at this last attempt to escape.

He started on the room, tearing it apart uncertainly, not sure if she was here or had somehow gotten by him in the utter blackness. He pulled drawers onto the floor, emptied them. She felt the pressure of the bed as his weight shifted across it. She stifled the urge to cry out, biting on her hand again.

His hand reached under the bed, hovered close to her for an eternity, felt the carpet next to her face. She held her breath, sensed the hand searching, coming closer . . . Until she was sure it had retreated.

He's blind, Faith thought. He can't see anything.

The storm raged around her for long minutes, and in her silence she said an eulogy for Albert. It was enough to keep her mind off Rain as he stalked the room. A prayer for his lost soul. To Heaven you go, my young friend, to your parents.

And then he left the bedroom.

She didn't know why, or even if he had really gone. Was he waiting, still playing his game? A trick to draw her into the open. She didn't dare move.

She waited, but knew that if she remained under the bed he would eventually find her. It might take minutes or hours, but he would discover her hiding place and kill her.

The only way she was going to survive this night, Faith decided, was to fight back and get out of the house.

She noiselessly crawled from under the bed, into the wreck of a now unfamiliar room. She wondered if his eyes were fixed to her even then. Watching. Waiting to strike her down like the lightning that ripped to the ground, ravaging the sky to the sound of crashing thunder.

Stopping The Rain

The scrambler kicked up dirt and jumped down an embankment. They both nearly fell off and the engine revved under the din of the storm after they had regained their balance. Will struggled to keep the bike upright, Veronica clinging to him without the confidence she had yielded when she was on the vehicle with Albert. From here, Will could see a car in front of the property.

Rain was already there!

They raced on, skidding and sliding, losing control and regaining it before they crashed.

Then, suddenly, he brought the bike to a halt. He wanted so much to ride up to the house but knew that if Rain heard the engine, he wouldn't hesitate in killing Faith. He remembered something she had told him when he had been an eager detective back in Denver, looking to save lives.

He likes to play games.

Will climbed from the scrambler. Let her still be alive, he prayed. Rain wouldn't kill her straight away, but would torture her first. He had to get to the house before she suffered.

'Fetch Sheriff Nash,' he told Veronica urgently.

'But I've never—'

'Just keep your balance and don't crash.'

'Shall I come in with you?' she cried, her face dirty.

'No – just get Sheriff Nash. Go!' he shouted over the storm and set off, running as fast as he could.

'Good luck!' he heard her call, and then the engine faded into the horrible night.

He neared the fencing around the property and paused for breath.

His tired heart lurched when the only light on in the house blinked out.

Climbing over the perimeter, he continued on, breathless. Tripped, twisted his ankle.

'Keep going,' he encouraged himself, the stitch he had developed digging at his insides like the point of a knife. He pulled himself up and hobbled on, wincing with pain. *'Come on!'*

In Denver, when Dominick Rain was playing his sick game with Tabitha Warner, Faith had said that it was over very quickly. Once the man – for that was all he was, not a monster – reached a breaking point in his fucked-up psychology then the game was over, leaving only a frenzy of pain to the loser.

It's over very quickly.

Will Bradley prayed to God that Rain hadn't snapped yet, that Faith was still alive. That he had not let her die . . .

The Kitchen

It was the most fearful gauntlet Faith had ever run, and the slowest. She had made it all the way to the kitchen, crawling stealthily through disorder and confusion, disorientated in her own home, fighting to keep her bearings in the mess. Her whole house had been tilted on its side, every content of every nook, cranny and cupboard poured into the open spaces. More junk than she ever cared to own – all of it now obstacles hindering her escape.

She didn't stand up because she believed it was safer at ground level. If he did find her, it would be by accident. He'd literally stumble over her rather than spotting her in the dark. If that happened she would grab the nearest object and attack him with it, bash him until she found his skull, crack it open and end his reign of terror that had lasted almost two decades.

The most frightening moments were when he was silent. His frantic search ceased, as he gathered himself for the next rage. His noise was also cover for any sounds she might make. She prayed that he was not watching her, smiling. He could even have followed her all the way here, letting her feel hope, a part of his revolting game. She wouldn't know it, if his cold hands were about to reach out and touch her.

She halted once inside the kitchen.

It had taken her ten minutes to reach here from the bedroom, and now she was only one room away from the exit – the outside world and freedom. But he was silent once more, and she imagined him stalking her from room to room. Or watching, staring, a knife in his hand. About to grab her, hold her, ensure she didn't escape.

Faith was sure she could feel his breathing on the back of her neck.

She began to crawl again, this time seeking a new hiding place.

201

She needed to rest, sensed she had been extremely lucky to survive this long, and that her luck had to change soon.

Then she found the stove and crept into the narrow gap between it and the fridge. As she shrank into the dead-end crawlspace, she hoped the moon was hidden behind thick clouds. Keeping her safe . . .

Two eyes watched her hide.

The fridge door had been left open when she had answered the door, and now she was bathed in an angelic glow. Despite her fearful expression, she looked beautiful.

The man smiled, grateful that he had finally found her.

Faith tried not to make a sound, listening to the footfalls get louder, the man getting closer, seemingly on a direct route for her. Staying here had not been clever; she should have made for the door and—

Suddenly a strong hand grabbed her arm, and pulled her firmly from the space. She tried to scream, but his other hand clamped over her mouth. She wriggled frantically, trying to kick him, punch him, scratch his eyes out, but he was too strong.

'Come with me if you want to live,' he told her, and removed his hand from her mouth.

'Will?' she gasped, hugged him. *'Oh, Will . . .'*

'Yes, it's me. Christ I've missed you,' he said, and quickly kissed her. 'Now we have to go,' he instructed urgently.

As Will turned, he walked straight onto the knife that Dominick Rain pushed viciously into his gut. Rain removed the blade quickly and Will fell to his knees, shocked, holding the bloody wound in both hands, letting go of Faith.

'Will?' she trembled, hearing the terrible sounds.

'Go,' he groaned. 'Go to the basement . . .' He was gurgling blood, spitting it out, coughing, as the knife penetrated his stomach again. *'Basement.'*

Will remembered the details of Rain's case as he collapsed – the awful story of a child held captive in squalor for over a decade, down in a pit of a room, a cellar especially excavated. If Faith could only get down there, Rain might not follow. He might be afraid. It was her only hope.

'You should have ended it when you had a chance,' Rain sneered, 'on the roof of the Institute. But you were weak. I will be strong. I will survive this night, and the next, to kill them all.'

Rain approached swiftly and the knife came in again. Feebly, Will did his best to deflect the blade, and caught it in his shoulder.

'Run,' he croaked, but Faith wouldn't move from his side; she was unable to leave him now they were together again. '*Run!*' he screamed, the knife coming in again.

He ducked and it glanced off his ear. He screamed in agony, felt his ear dangling from a tether of skin. The pain was overwhelming and he wanted to pass out, but he had to stay and fight.

He remembered as a detective looking into the soulless eyes of so many murder victims, wishing for a way to bring them back. All he ever wanted was to save those who were going to die before their time, and now, finally, he had his chance.

For Faith . . .

He reached up, grabbing at Rain. Faith had left the kitchen, crying his name, and Will knew he might have to die if she was to survive this night. He had to preoccupy Rain for as long as possible. This time he managed to shield the knife with his arm, but felt it swiping flesh away. He shouted in defiance and rage, fighting, hanging on, the other man stronger, still wielding his blade. This time it deflected off his palm, slicing it open.

'Come on!' Will screamed, but could feel consciousness slipping away. He was falling, darkness encompassing him. Down into an empty void . . .

Rain left him.

The knife was no longer piercing Bradley's flesh; the agony of his wounds now prevailing. He closed his eyes, keeled over in his own blood, his last conscious thought a hope that he would see Faith again one day. Would hold her hand, and whisper his love.

The Boy

Faith staggered down the wooden stairs, almost falling twice. A wave of horror and loss and sadness washed over her; she felt like she was drowning under her own private tsunami as she began to rummage through the unopened boxes and parcels for anything she could use as a weapon.

As she touched each item, a bolt of energy charged her heart.

A fifteen-year-old raped by her boyfriend, shooting her assailant with her father's gun . . . A young couple defying their parents to remain together, even if it meant moving away, not staying in touch . . . A kid involved in a robbery, a dead pregnant woman . . . A child. A dead child. Buried in the back of a . . . A husband cheating on his wife with her sister . . . A man who liked . . . A boy who . . . An old lady . . .

She listened to their fears and worries, but then the door burst open at the top of the stairs. She still didn't have a weapon.

Why had Will sent her down here? Why had she listened when she could have made it to the door? He must have had a reason. He couldn't have known about all the lost emotions she kept down here.

She clutched a baseball bat, hearing his first step down. The wood creaked. He stopped.

'Going to get you,' he whispered. 'I'm not afraid to go down there.'

He was scared, she realised. He didn't want to come into the basement. Will knew. She prayed he was still alive. Wished she could reach out with the power to comfort him.

Faith hid in the darkness under the stairs, gripping the bat tightly . . . *watching a boy who liked to play baseball. He would be the first on the diamond, the last off. He helped the coach to gather*

204

the bats and balls because he loved the touch of the smooth wood, the scent of the game. His battered, tattered mitt and this bat were his most treasured possessions. The coach beckoned him over as he put the equipment back in the cage.

The coach waved him over. They were alone. Everybody else long gone. She concentrated on the two, out where it was safe, away from the serial killer. Trying not to think of Will bleeding upstairs, dying, but the boy. Always the boy . . .

Running to the coach, cheerful smile. The coach removes his cap and leads the boy into his office. The man is sweating when he locks the door, tells the boy to undress —

She almost dropped the bat.

'Dominick,' she called, sensing him hovering above. She could no longer take sanctuary in the bat, not after what the coach had done to his favourite player. She renewed her grip, white-knuckle tight. That poor boy, every fortnight, the man raping him.

'Dominick, come down here to me.'

She had to fight back.

Roadside

In the glare of the headlights, Veronica strained to hold up her hand, trapped under the weight of the scrambler.

The vehicle stopped and Sheriff Nash climbed out. She rushed to the teenager.

'You OK?' she asked, lifting the bike off.

'Albert's dead,' the young woman sobbed.

'Can you move?'

'I think so.'

Louise helped the kid to her feet and they made it back to the Maverick. 'Hold on,' Louise said, slamming the four by four into drive.

'He said to tell you the blind woman is in danger,' Veronica babbled, crying. 'I was going to get help but came off the bike. Is he really gone?'

'Hush,' the Sheriff soothed, putting a hand on her leg. 'You're in shock. Stay calm.'

Hold on, Faith, Louise thought. Stay alive for a few minutes longer.

The Lost Children – Three

Dominick waited uncertainly at the top of the basement steps, peering into the darkness, unsure of what lay below. He remembered his childhood, years beneath a house like this one, in a windowless room without daylight, Lorna – his sister – his eternal companion. He wondered if this was a trap, the blind woman used as bait, so that they could hold him here again, and never let him back into the real world except to do their bidding . . .

Sometimes, Ethan Wallace would cruise the night roads, searching for hitch-hikers to take back to the house. He'd offer them amenities, every comfort of home. A place out of the cold and rain. A bed for the night. Ethan called it bringing his work back home with him.

Juliet Stevens didn't like the idea of having strangers in their home, the old farm; she was worried by what they might do or find. 'Drifters,' Ethan explained to her one night. 'Nobody knows where they've come from, or where they are heading to. Perfect for us,' he smiled.

So the kindly young couple would offer a bed for the night, a breakfast with the rising sun. Sometimes the drifters died in their sleep and they didn't have to bother cooking anything the next morning.

Other times they would wake and dress and eat heartily, questioning their hosts about unusual sounds in the night, which Juliet didn't think was very polite.

Damndest thing – thought I heard a child crying last night. Didn't know you sweethearts had offspring. Where do you keep the little critters?

There was usually a mess. Ethan had never learned how to kill cleanly, and now that Juliet couldn't see he didn't recognise the need. Besides, the kids could always clean up.

Ethan would drag the boy upstairs and make him scrub and wash all the blood away. Every pale fleck of skin and hank of hair.

You gotta clean this mess up, boy.

If his son cried or complained, kicked or struggled, Ethan would blindfold him and lead him to the red-tiled kitchen.

Stop your bitching. This is how Mother gets by. You have to help her clean this place up.

If Ethan and Juliet still felt like having a good time, they would strip the boy naked, smear blood all over him.

What is that? Can you guess?

Touch brain-matter to his cheeks, make him taste it, then describe the flavour. Laugh at him when he vomited and then make him clean that up, too.

Want to play some more?

They would dispose of the latest body, taking whatever money, clothing and other personal effects they desired, leaving the rest to rot with the buried corpse.

Then they'd push the boy back down to their daughter – Lorna, who thought she was so clever always trying to figure out what made the world go round.

If there were no drifters to be found, no unsuspecting victims, they would bring the children up, and torture their little minds.

Children can be fun, after all . . .

Dominick, sweating, stared around.

He was alone and Faith Gallagher was down in the basement. He had to get her.

He took one step. Stopped. Made sure his parents were not about to lock him in. He remembered Lorna explaining that he had killed them, set himself and her free from the pit for ever. But what if she was wrong? Another slow step. He nodded. Lifted his foot. Keep going, he told himself firmly. They were dead.

'Dominick,' Lorna called from the dark pit beneath him. *That can't be.* He had set her free. They had been held without choice

208

or ransom, and after years they had escaped. She couldn't be here. He looked around, checking for his parents. 'Dominick, come down here to me.'

Dominick had to save her, get her out of here. He quickly ran down, his feet pounding loudly.

Faith waited under the stairs, breathing deeply, silently. It was time to fight back.

Don't swing the bat early, she thought, listening to his descent, and she gripped the baseball bat tighter, repulsed . . . *The coach forcing himself upon the small figure of the boy . . .*

When she heard his feet pounding directly in front of her, the old wood creaking heavily, she swung the bat as hard as she could, saw the boy doing the same, cracking the coach's head wide open. She used his strength. Her blow shattered the rotted wooden banister, and broke Rain's ankle on contact.

Dominick screamed and fell, tumbling and splitting his head open when it impacted on the hard ground.

Faith remained still, listening to him breathe, trying to decipher any sounds that would show he was coming for her. She had to get out of there. She had to reach Will, find out if he was still alive. Hoping that he had not died for her.

She felt for the banister. There was no change in Rain's breathing. She had taken just one step up the stairs when, suddenly, a hand grabbed her leg.

Faith screamed.

He was pulling her back down and she fell, grabbing for the wooden banister. She rolled over, reached for him and found his face. Panting, terrified, she clawed his eyes. He screamed, but still held her while she ripped at his eyes with her nails.

He jerked back in agony and she was free. Gasping, she began to haul herself up the stairs.

'Get down!' Louise called, and Faith dropped to her knees, providing the Sheriff with a clear shot.

Dominick Rain was clambering up behind her, sure he had almost reached the bitch although he could no longer see. Blood was leaking profusely from his eyes. He was blind. And then he was gone, falling back down the stairs at an explosion of sound.

Weeping, traumatised, Faith stumbled up the stairs to Will, who lay motionless in a pool of blood on the kitchen floor. Louise fixed dressings on his wounds as best she could before the paramedics arrived. When they did, Louise went down into the basement, her gun raised and ready to fire, half-expecting Rain to be mysteriously gone.

But he was still there, his body twisted and wrecked. One eye was hanging from its socket by a fine tether of gore, the other merely caked with blood.

Louise bent over him, wondering what had made him this way. What dark forces in the world could take a decent soul and mould it to serve evil without purpose? What had happened to him as a child that could have turned him this way? Or had he been born this way . . . Unwanted tears slipped from her eyes. She had never killed anybody before, and never would again.

She lifted his shirt and looked for the scar Will Bradley had told her about. As she touched it, she wondered if all this would have happened in her town, had she listened to the former detective and taken immediate action.

Louise Nash walked slowly out of the basement, Faith Gallagher's wrecked, bloody house, and into the still desert. She stood under the stars she owned with Wade and looked up at them. The stars they would share for ever.

EPILOGUE

The True Spirit

The True Spirit

'You came for me, Will,' Faith told him, gripping his hand tightly. *'Don't leave me now.'*

The question of whether Will Bradley would live or die was a touch-and-go matter. He was yet to regain consciousness.

Faith sat beside his hospital bed, keeping vigil until the moment he woke, watching over him and praying for his soul – praying that he wouldn't leave her alone in the dark now that they had found each other again.

She listened to the constant beeping of the monitoring equipment, lulling her into fitful bouts of sleep because that was his heart, *alive*, each sound an affirmation of his love, the reason he had come to her. If he did die – he wouldn't, *couldn't*, she thought fearfully – she would always know that despite their years apart they had always been thinking of each other, loving from a distance, that he had chosen to find her and that they would have been together until the very end.

She dozed, afraid to let in a single bleak thought, feeling that somehow he would tune into it and lose hope, lose the will to fight back. Instead she dreamed of pleasant times, of setting up a home and having a family . . . and when she woke it was to the tight grip of his hand.

'Nurse!' Faith called. 'Nurse! He's awake!' She turned, leaned close to him. 'Will? I'm here.'

His eyes opened, looked at her.

'Always,' he whispered, lips dry. His free hand touched his heart. *'Always.'*

'Will,' she sobbed. 'I love you.'

His eyes closed and his hand slowly began to relinquish its tight grip.

'Will?'

He let go and his hand fell to the bed.

'Nurse! Dr Bale!' Faith screamed. 'Please, Will! Don't leave me.'

She could hear their pounding feet coming down the corridor. They sounded miles off. *Hurry*. The lullaby beeping of machines that had sent her to sleep so often over the past couple of days now turned into an elongated screech of pain.

Faith searched for his hand, sensed his fingers close around hers for a fleeting moment.

'Don't go,' she whispered, but his hand drifted away again. 'Please, Will, please don't leave me, not now,' she begged, cradling his hand.

Two years later, having left Cradle in the hands of Deputy James Kennedy and found more fulfilling work searching for missing children when she set up the Hope Agency, Louise gave birth to a little baby boy.

Cradling his newborn son in his arms, looking at the little face with tears in his eyes, Wade was in awe, thought he might never have seen anything quite so beautiful as the sight in that room. They had decided to name him Will, after the dead private investigator. They had spoken to Faith – a good friend – and asked her to be his godmother.

The next evening, Wade went to Louise's room and helped her into a wheelchair.

'Wade, what are you doing now?' she asked. 'I can walk, you know.'

'Sit back and enjoy the ride. I have something to show you.'

He gained permission from a nurse, found an exit and pushed her outside, to the small gardens at the centre of the hospital complex. He eased her from the chair and together they lay on their backs, looking at the clear night sky.

Beneath the stars.

Wade hugged her, held her, and they watched in silence until a star fell to Earth.

'Starlight, starbright, burning through the sky tonight. I wish I may, I wish I might, have this wish, I wish tonight,' he whispered.

'What did you wish for?' she asked softly, holding his hand.

'If I tell, it won't ever come true,' he smiled.

'It might.'

'I don't know . . .' he hesitated.

'Tell me,' she demanded.

'Will you marry me, Louise Nash?' he asked her, staring at their stars.

'Maybe,' she grinned. 'Maybe not. I'll tell you in the morning. Now be quiet and stop ruining this moment.'

At the back of the hospital, underneath the blanket of night and the stars they owned, they decided to marry. They didn't need priests or rings, or witnesses. No wedding finery or fancy catering. They had each other, and that was enough.

Always.

Lorna Cole spent many months watching Faith Gallagher reconstruct her life after Will Bradley's death at the hand of her brother. She studied the blind woman trawl through misery, as she endured her own bereavement, and contemplated killing her many times.

The final occasion was on the day Faith was married, four years after the shooting in the basement.

She watched the scene outside the church where the wedding guests were gathered, staring through the electronic scope of the powerful rifle, wondering how Faith's gorgeous white dress would look, spattered with her blood. She hated the other woman. Then she shifted her aim, passing Louise Nash and her husband Wade, focusing on the husband-to-be – a jazz-band player named Danny Glickman. They had met in a bar when Faith offered to buy him a drink after listening to the dulcet tones he created with his saxophone. Heart-rending music that reminded her of Will.

Faith had stolen Dominick away, Lorna thought ferociously, put her beloved brother, her lover, her other self, in a grave. Now she would give Faith the same pain. Kill the man *she* loved.

Her finger on the sensitive trigger, she began to apply pressure, looking down into the courtyard.

Then she stopped, a hair's breadth from shooting.

If she pulled the trigger, put a hole in his head, where would that lead?

She had always condoned Dominick's deviant behaviour. This

215

vengeance would seduce her into more killing, would take her along a similar path. After all, hadn't the blind psychic suffered enough? She, too, had lost the man she loved, and through no fault of her own.

There was too much pain and misery in the world, Lorna decided. Yes, Dominick was gone . . . But so too were Will Bradley, Agent Jack Ramsey and poor Albert Dreyfuss, along with all the murdered blind women, and their own parents, Ethan and Juliet.

Somebody had to put a stop to all the horror.

Her vision blurred as she looked once more through the scope. Prepared to fire again.

She lowered the rifle and wiped her wet eyes.

If she did kill Faith, or Danny Glickman who knew nothing of this, all those years caring for Dominick in the cellar would have been wasted. All the years reading and studying down in the dark . . . her passion and desire to become a decent human being. All that compassion, just so that she could follow her brother into the black abyss of death after she had survived their harrowing childhood.

She looked up at the deep blue sky, the delicate white clouds, the surrounding majesty that she could almost reach out and touch from the roof. She was reminded of the day they had come out of the farmhouse together, teenagers, for the first and final time, leaving behind them two buried bodies. Dominick had been in such awe of the blue ceiling to the world.

She relived that moment now and began to cry. There was a new world ahead now, as there had been all those years ago. And she had to choose between two very different paths, as she had when she was a young woman in an unfamiliar place.

She had made the right choice then, but had gotten lost on her journey. Now she wanted to get back on the right path, the path of a true spirit. Learn again the truth of what being human meant.

Confetti decorated the sky like snow and she put the rifle down.

'Happily ever after,' she whispered. Just like the fairy tales she used to read to Dominick by candlelight.

And walked away, to her own happiness.